Y0-DDS-920

Christmas '06
For Looty + Poulette
"Finally ... my mother's son..."
lofa ato
VOB

SPLIT CREEK

Also by V.O. Blum

EQUATOR: THE STORY AND THE LETTERS

SUNBELT STORIES

SPLIT CREEK

WAR NOVEL OF THE DEEP WEST

V.O. BLUM

Foreword by Roger J. Porter

TIMES EAGLE BOOKS
ASTORIA, OREGON

Copy Editors: Jefferson Ranck (English);
  Christel Jonge Vos (German)
Front cover design: Arnold Pander
Back cover design: Peggy Lindquist
Production and text design: Peggy Lindquist

Set in Janson type
Printed in the United States of America
First Edition: January 2007
Published by Times Eagle Books, Astoria, OR 97103
  www.timeseaglebooks.com
Member, PMA—the Independent Book Publishers
  Association

Library of Congress Cataloging-in-Publication Number:
  2004-1955 73
International Standard Book Number:
  0-9620886-3-3
ISBN 13: 978-0-9620886-3-6

Acknowledgments

The author is grateful for advice received from locals regarding wartime life in the Deep West[1]. Key sources were warned this novel would significantly depart from historical fact. All respected this license—that is, none conditioned assistance on learning what sort of tale might be spun. Hopefully, none will conclude trust was misplaced.

Thanks, then, to:

Amber Johns of Northeastern Nevada Museum (Elko, Nevada) for archival assistance regarding the derailment of the *City of San Francisco* by alleged saboteurs in 1939 (See Historical Postscript);

The Wyoming Room of Fulmer Library (Sheridan, Wyoming) for bibliographic assistance regarding German POWs in the Deep West (1943-46);

Charlie Gould of Just Gone Fishing (Buffalo, Wyoming) for tips on fly fishing; Randy Kouf, formerly of CSI Outdoor Products (Sheridan, Wyoming), for pointers on elk hunting; Zane Garstad of Sheridan College (Sheridan) for rodeo technique; and Tom Ringley of Memorial Hospital Foundation (Sheridan) for rodeo history;

[1] By Deep West is meant Arizona, Colorado, Idaho, Montana, Nevada, New Mexico, Utah, and Wyoming.

Lynwood Tallbull of North Cheyenne Elderly (Lame Deer, Montana) for descriptions of Native American medicine; Alfred High Horse for advice about Native American language on the Plains; and John Heriard of Written Heritage (Folsom, Louisiana) for historical information regarding Native American dance in the Deep West;

German-Russian immigrants to the Clear Creek Valley (Clearmont and Ucross, Wyoming)[2]—and their spouses and descendants—for recollections of sugar agronomy and the deployment of German prisoners on valley ranches and farms,[3] such sources including, Dollie Brug Iberlin (co-author of *The White Root*—see Further Reading), William Leis, Richard Lenz, Le Ora Pitsch, and Donald Schuman. The author also consulted an interview with Ruth Fowler, Alek Kaufmann, Ralph Kaiser, and Alex Pitsch conducted by a Sheridan County extension agent in 1987. Among these patriotic U.S. families was the young war hero, Robert T. Wagner, reportedly executed by Nazi Germany after being captured on an intelligence

---

[2] On her accession in 1762, Russia's Catherine II invited her former (German) compatriots to settle in the Volga River Valley; they began to lose their contractual rights, however, under the reign of Alexander II (r. 1855-81). Emigration accelerated in the late 19th century, with some families settling the Clear Creek Valley after World War I.

[3] Branch Camp #7 of Camp Scottsbluff (Scottsbluff, Nebraska) was located in Clearmont during the summer of 1945, housing some 250 German prisoners. In the autumn, the facility became a branch camp of Camp Douglas (Douglas, Wyoming) and housed some 200 German prisoners.

mission along the Rhine River.

The author is also grateful to the following German-Americans:

The late Prof. Horst Duhnke, of California State University at Hayward, for guidance regarding imperfect data about the German Communist Party under the Nazi regime; and Prof. Ottomar Rudolf of Reed College (Portland, Oregon) and Hans Crome, previously of the College Preparatory School (Oakland, California), for their recollections of Hitler Youth—both are now committed democrats.

And former German POWs Henry Kemper (Portland, Oregon) and Fred Wolff (Kensington, California) for their recollections of internment in the U.S.—both are now committed democrats.

And thanks to the ranch hands of the Ucross Foundation's Big Red Ranch (Ucross, Wyoming) for sharing the ranch's wartime history during the author's literary residency in the spring of '87. Like some other ranches and farms in the valley, Big Red deployed German prisoners from June-November 1945. It was acquired by the Foundation in '82 and hosted its first group of artists (both literary and fine) the following year.

Here in Oregon, the author is grateful for key literary advice from Walt Curtis, David A. Horowitz, Karen Irwin, Arnold Pander, and, of course, the Times Eagle team—Michael P. McCusker, Candice Crossley, and, in the Bay Area, Katryn Snow; and during production, appreciated the hospitality of David A. Horowitz and Gloria E. Myers.

V.O.B.
Arch Cape, Oregon
October 2006

In Memoriam

For the estimated 5000 sons and daughters of the Deep West who sacrificed their lives in the war against European fascism (1942-45)

Foreword

Roger J. Porter

When we think of American penal institutions housing enemy prisoners of war, Guantanamo comes to mind, though of course that facility is not on American soil but on a naval base leased from Cuba. Yet long before terrorist suspects were shipped off to cages in the Western Hemisphere, in circumstances unfamiliar to most Americans enemy combatants were incarcerated in the U.S. heartland. During World War II almost 400,000 German POWs were confined in some 150 detention camps, largely in the South, the Southwest, the Plains states, and the Mountain states. Perhaps equally surprising, those prisoners for the most part were extremely well-treated and with great tolerance, considering we were at war with their country; they experienced a freedom unparalleled for inmates of war camps. While many of them worked in agriculture and small manufacturing—a far more benign version of *"Arbeit Macht Frei"*—they had rather cushy accommodations at their disposal: canteens, infirmaries, libraries, post offices, laundries; even gyms, tennis courts, and theaters. (One of the American neighbors of *Split Creek*'s Camp Roberts refers to the facility as "The Fritz Ritz.") Because, according to the Geneva Convention, officers were not required to work, most of those men passed their time in recreational, cultural, and educational programs. It will probably astonish Americans to know that activities in the camps included the writing of democratic newspapers, stocking libraries with books banned and burned by the Nazis, lectures, a camp chorus and musical evenings, even a cabaret. Thomas Mann was a featured author in discussion groups at many such camps. If our image of Guantanamo prisoners is that of shackled, orange-suited, and broken men, our image of the captives from the Wehrmacht—at least of the officers—ought to be of men under minimal supervision and who, with some liberty to come and go as they chose, were frequently welcomed into the surrounding communities, especially where the local citizens possessed German ancestry. One wag at the time said that the best way to have a good war is to be on the losing side, get captured, and then be shipped off to a prison camp in the U.S.

The population of the detention centers often split between a diehard Nazi minority and a non-Nazi majority. Though we might be inclined to imagine these camps as hotbeds of Nazism, such was not necessarily the case, and many of the prisoners during their stay became enamored of American democracy; some, unwillingly conscripted into the German army, were already prone to believe in American—or at least in democratic and humanitarian—values. These prisoners tended to regard the Allies not as their enemies but as their supporters in helping to eradicate Nazism. There were numerous staunch opponents of the Nazi regime, many of whom propagandized fellow inmates to oppose Hitler, though fervent Nazis terrorized their more liberal comrades by sending back home "black lists" of anti-Nazis for possible retribution by the regime against their families. A democratic spirit flourished in a camp in Massachusetts (where else?), when, in 1944, anti-Nazi prisoners established a "Prisoner of War Council for a Democratic Germany" with an agenda that included support for the investigation of Nazi war crimes—especially the persecution of the Jews—and a free democratic press in Germany. One anti-Nazi soldier wrote from that camp in 1945:

> In this land of liberty I found everything I was looking for: humanity, fair treatment, justice; but I didn't find a chance for activity against the beasts who were going to destroy my own people and others...

To avoid the tensions stirred up by opposing ideologies among the prisoners, a number of designated anti-Nazi German POW camps were established. Many of the German dissidents were from the Africa Corps, the Division in which the hero of V.O. Blum's novel, Lieutenant Friedrich Dassen, served.

The novel's title *Split Creek* becomes a metaphor for the ideological fractures in Dassen. Torn between loyalty to the Communism championed by his beloved mother, German nationalism in its less malignant version (early on he rejects Nazism and fascism), and a humane democratic ideal (championed by one of his heroes John Stuart Mill), Dassen declares "I'd lived the sickle, the swastika, the stars 'n' stripes." This is a classic *bildungsroman* or coming of age novel, told in the first person by Dassen as he recalls his life in Germany and then in the prison camp where he spent the late years of the war. The autobiographical protagonist looks back from the vantage point of 1992 on his long life, surveying choices foisted upon him and those he has elected, often with considerable risk. As a young boy he sees his mother taken away and confined for her pro-Soviet allegiance and activities; finds himself forced against his will to serve in the Hitler Youth; gets conscripted into a German army unit in North Africa with a mission to sabotage Allied oil lines; and finally is captured and transported to a POW camp in the American West.

Here his troubles really begin. Dassen is befriended by Bud Hoffman, a rancher who not only has German roots but is a vehement American fascist convinced Jews have plunged us into war with Germany; Bud wants nothing more than that his daughter Helen sire a German child. Virtually pimping for his equally pro-Nazi daughter, to whom the naive and sex-starved Friedrich is deeply attracted, Bud applauds when she becomes pregnant with Friedrich's child, whom she calls her "Aryan Warrior," much to Dassen's chagrin.

The story is narrated by Dassen in his seventies. We know little about his life between 1944 and 1992, when the last section takes place, other than that he has become a Professor of European History at Cal State Hayward; that he, good American Democrat, has voted for Stevenson, Carter, and Clinton; and that the "Warrior," whom Dassen thought dead, has survived. That son Thor, now forty-eight, visits the old man to announce his existence. He is a kind of mercenary soldier in a professional military company with Christian values and, his mother's genes intact, is a virulent anti-semite to boot, painful news to his father who muses "the Warrior was my nemesis."

Where do we find the center of gravity (or of gravitas) in this novel? In political terms, it seems to be a celebration of American liberalism, largely in its anti-authoritarian forms as well as its optimism regarding openness, progress, and the belief that one is never confined to the conventions and determinations of the past, whether national, familial, or personal. Dassen embodies the belief that change is always possible, that the dead hand of inheritance can be overthrown. In a key passage, he concludes that "Germany must be purged of National Socialism, then revived as a democracy." "Yankee kindness" helps grease the tracks to an Edenic America: "I came Nazi, I left free." It's a simple creed, and Blum treats his protagonist in a straightforward, non-ironic fashion. In many ways not only the setting of this work but its deepest ethos is that of "the good war" and the democratic triumph arising from that history; Blum clearly writes under the sway of the values that defeated European totalitarianism.

Even the villain of the book endorses a heartland purity, and Bud, taking Friedrich hiking, hunting, and fishing, sounds like a would-be Hemingway. And while we might question Friedrich's easy use of slang (how *did* he learn to say "binos" for binoculars, "calm down, cowboy," "bagged" for caught [fish]?), his avid use of American-isms suggests that the protagonist's entry into the vernacular functions largely to endorse our national values, at least circa 1945.

Dassen loves myth and metaphor, especially when they serve to characterize his adopted country, and they are never in short supply: employing a metaphor for his mother's resistance to the culture of Nazism that threatens to destroy her, Friedrich imagines her as a Plains Indian disdaining the White Man's civilization. He regards Helen as "the fascist queen," but in his eyes she also represents the possibilities of his new situation, a transition to his future opportunities. When I read the sex scenes, I think of the poet John Donne's ecstatic address to his mistress: "Oh my America! my new-found-land." Dassen's therapist (what could be more American than giving a political prisoner a shrink?) offers him a book by Norman Thomas, and she is adamant that the great Socialist be considered a democrat as well; in this passage Thomas is more American than the Americans.

And yet there's a German intellectual strain throughout the novel, which sometimes seems to clash with the emphasis on American innocence. Balancing the camp's nativist indoctrination program, which urges the prisoners "Have fun with democracy" and combine "democracy and baseball," we have frequent lectures on the course of European civilization. Dassen is steeped in European philosophy, and he makes references to

Goethe, Heidegger, Holderin, Descartes, Mill, Marx, Trotsky, and Nietzsche. Even the egregious Bud delivers a lengthy discourse on Hebraism and Hellenism, replete with allusions to Heraclitus, Galileo, Newton, Leibniz, Shakespeare, and Racine. There are debates about Marxism, essays on anti-semitism, footnotes citing instances of German sabotage in the U.S. and mini-histories of fascism in America, and references to Mill's theories of meritocracy. Blum's heart occasionally seems as much in the treatise and the tract as in the story.

But in the end *Split Creek* remains profoundly American…and let me be speculative and surmise the reason Blum has, at this historical moment, chosen to tell this tale. I believe the author looks back to "the good war" if not with nostalgia then with a painful awareness of the contrast between that enterprise and the misguided idealism that drives the current administration and its tragic adventure in Iraq. The long, complex journey that Dassen takes in his route to citizenship entitles him to stand up against the son whose attitudes resonate with past horrors. Thor is the dark side of America, various incarnations of which we have seen in the past decade; and Dassen's denunciation of him, coming from a man who espouses the Enlightenment and a rational humanism, is meant in some sense to cleanse America itself of its grave errors. Bud drinks to his daughter's unborn child who will "lead us from the Morass" and "forge the New Order," and when we finally encounter this phony messiah I suspect we are meant to see in him a version of right-wing religious fanaticism that seriously threat-

American freedom. In contending with his son as .e contended with his fatherland, Dassen becomes the advocate of the best that America might be.

Roger J. Porter is professor of English Literature and Humanities at Reed College. A noted critic of autobiography, he is author of Self-Same Songs: Autobiographical Performances and Reflections *(University of Nebraska, 2002) and co-author of* The Voice Within *(Knopf, 1973). Among other journals, his criticism has appeared in* Sewanee Review, Hudson Review, *and* Massachusetts Review.

SPLIT CREEK

Töten ist eine Gestalt unseres wandernden Trauerns…
Rein ist im heiteren Geist,
Was an uns selber geschieht.

Killing is a form of our wandering grief…
Clarity occurs to us within serene spirit.

Sonnets to Orpheus
Rainer Maria Rilke
February 1922

Part One

1918-44

1

My father was the last German soldier to die in the First World War. His squadron was defending a hillside in Belgium when a Canadian platoon surprised them at dawn. The Armistice was announced later that morning. That night my mother celebrated the peace with comrades in Berlin. They were confident of a communist future—an *Umsturz* that would depose the bourgeois order.

A comrade who worked at the wire service noticed Father's name in a dispatch called "Germany's Last Heroes." He bicycled over with the news. In the hallway, after a silence, Mother accepted Father's death with irony. "In my heart I always knew he was a phantom. There were times I would stare at him to convince myself he was real. I never persuaded myself."

"Nor the Reaper, Helga."

She pointed to me—Friedrich the Embryo. Her voice quivered. "The child will never—"

"But the child will know *you*, Helga." He embraced her while she sobbed.

I was born the following June, the product of Father's last furlough. He'd been given two weeks and they'd gone to the Alps. It rained the day I was conceived.

My first memory is dancing the tango for the Labor

Committee of the Party. They'd just planned the steel strike of 1923. Comrade Maslow tapped the rhythm with his pen. The gramophone scratched, the floor squeaked.

Mother split her time between her studio on the Kantplatz, where she designed dresses, and the Party. The union leaders—even the socialist ones—treasured her: she knew exactly when to scold the bosses and call the strike. She won four of her actions, a fact the Nazis never forgot.

The first time I saw a swastika was outside Heine Library—two youths were handing out flyers condemning the Versailles Treaty. I was only eleven—their arrogance frightened me. I asked Mother if the Nazis would win. She tightened her grip of my hand as we crossed the street. "Not while I'm alive, *Junge*."

The next two years were eerie. While Germany languished, Mother prospered—her dresses were in vogue. Marlene Dietrich bought one and wore it in *Blonde Venus*.

I grew to be a stalwart youth, adored by my mother. I remember a summer day when I invited her to join me in the Wannsee. "No, swim, *Liebling*," she called back. "I'll watch you." That was how it was in those days—she preferred to watch rather than swim.

While we lived together, there was never a question of her remarrying or taking a lover. I don't mean to imply there was anything untoward between us. It's only that she remained as loyal to my father after his death as during his life, and, to her, I was his surviving spirit. "Just like your father," she would sigh, regarding my taste in music, wine…my goalie moves in soccer.

But oh my God, how Germany engulfed us! Prior to '33, we had money and the bliss of our mutual affection. What we didn't have was 38 percent of the electorate nor the respect of Hindenburg's son. That belonged to the Nazis.

"After a thirteen-year struggle the National Socialist movement has broken into the Government. But the struggle to win the Nation is only beginning." I remember Hitler's words crackling over the Blaupunkt that bright January morning. The announcer followed with Wagner. I looked at my mother accusingly: "You promised me!" I sulked. I was only thirteen, just a few months older than the Nazi Party itself.

She crushed a cigarette in the ashtray and grimaced. "You asked me whether they would win, Friedrich." She pushed the ashtray away. "All right, they've captured Germany. But they haven't won it." She contorted her face. "They *never* will."

I stated the obvious. "Mother. They *have*."

She slapped my face. "Germany isn't the whole world!" she cried sharply. "Never forget that!" She waved a finger at me. "DON'T FORGET THAT!"

The Gestapo came for her that spring—"protective custody," they called it. It wasn't in the middle of night, as legend might have it. It was on a Saturday morning in May. Her tulips had bloomed earlier that week. The officer had dated her best friend in the Lyzeum.

"*Ja*, I don't think it's so grave, Helga. They want you

5

old ones out of the way while they start their Labor Front."

"I'm not that old, Hermann."

He chuckled. "No, you're not. Just as beautiful as you were in school." She shot him a devilish glance that lasted only an instant. "Don't worry, Helga," he said softly. "You'll be out in a year or so."

He was partly right. The Nazis *did* murder Communists in the '30s—but only some five percent of the Party's 350,000 members. Nearly 150,000 others were sent to camps…though not just for a year. Most were released in '39 to make room for Jews, Gypsies, and Poles.

She pointed to me. "You'll take the boy to my sister?"

Hermann bowed. "Of course, Helga."

She scribbled the address, then latched her suitcase. She bowed before me and briskly stroked my hair. "All right, *Junge*, it's not the end of the world. Aunt Marie will take care of you." She swallowed. "I'll return."

I fought back tears. "When, Mother?"

"In time…In time."

I embraced her. "Good luck, Mama."

Aunt Marie and Uncle Martin were Communists too—they'd helped launch the Spartacists during the war. They had a small apartment by the Symphony. I slept on the sofa.

Mother was interned at Sachsenhausen which, like other camps, forbade visitors. But we received a letter every month. And although she wrote vaguely, we were able to guess the Party had infiltrated the camp and was able to improve conditions for members.

During her confinement, Mother never performed manual labor, and was soon rewarded with an office job. She slept in a bunker with three other women. During the warm months, she was permitted to join the staff exercise circle.

Although she never starved, her diet was tedious. "*Bohnen, Bohnen, Bohnen* [Beans, beans, beans]!" she complained in one of her letters. "One of these days I'll join the SS in return for a schnitzel!" Every month we packed a basket—cheese, fruit, sometimes even chocolate.

It was my lot to grow to manhood while Mother was in custody. By '36 Martin and Marie were insisting I conform. I remember Martin lighting his pipe after Sunday dinner. "Friedrich, you're a clever lad, and I know I can speak to you frankly."

"*Ja*, Uncle, of course."

He drew his pipe. Marie was in the kitchen. "These are terrible times—a nightmare, really…" He looked away from me.

"Uncle Martin?"

He forced himself to look back, then continued bravely. "*Ja*, well, because your mother is away, we're in a precarious position."

"Uncle, is my presence here…?"

He waved his hand. "No, no, you're just a lad—no danger to us at all." He looked me in the eyes. "But we must be sensible, *Bursche*."

"Have I done anything wrong?"

"On the contrary." He leaned forward. "It's not a question of what you've done, Friedrich, it's a question of

7

what you must do."

I braced myself. Would he ask me to betray Mother?

Marie was suddenly by Martin's side. "*Ja*, Friedrich, we must all be like the little animals in the woods now. You know, changing colors?"

"You mean 'camouflage'?" We were studying it in biology.

Martin laughed. "Yes, 'camouflage,' very good!" He smoked his pipe, hesitant to go on.

I broke the silence. "What must I do, uncle?"

He put his pipe down and spoke softly. "Well, they're talking about making *die Hitlerjugend* [Hitler Youth] compulsory."

I gasped. "Uncle! THEY WEAR SWASTIKAS!"

He and Marie stared at each other in horror.

♦

National Socialism pinned its hopes on German youth—to annihilate Judaism and Communism, impel imperialism, and entrench the totalitarian state. In a letter to Danzig's Nazi chief in '33, Hitler explained why the Party's future depended on the new generation:

> We older ones are used up. We are rotten to the marrow. We have no unrestrained instincts left. We are cowardly and sentimental. We bear the burden of a humiliating past and have in our blood the dull recollection of serfdom and servility…But my magnificent youngsters! Are there finer ones anywhere in the world? Look at these young men and boys! What material! With them I can make a new world!

At seventeen, I joined *HJ* to protect my uncle and aunt. It was customary to join in mid-April, on the eve of Hitler's birthday. I was inducted in our troop lodge, the cellar of a jewelry store. There was a poster of Hitler, an *HJ* flag, and a light bulb hanging from the ceiling. As a drum rolled and trumpet blared, I swore loyalty to *der Führer und unserer Fahne* [the Leader and our flag]. Then nearly fainted when I wrapped the swastika around my arm.

The platoon leader worried as I turned pale. "Are you all right, Dassen?" he gasped. He was younger than I was.

"It's a little exciting the first day, *mein Kameradschaftsführer* [my platoon leader]." A few lads smiled knowingly. There were 15 in the platoon, 30 in the troop.

Our first task was ecological—to collect paper and metal for recycling. Earlier in the year, I'd discovered an abandoned warehouse with copper wire on the shelves—my delivery of these spools made me a hero. Our second chore was philanthropic—collecting money for the Welfare Fund. Here again I was ingenious, finding a new library across the river from which to do my begging.

Troop activities were Wednesday and Saturday afternoons, plus every other Sunday. ("One for church, one for family, two for me," Hitler used to tell us.) Political class was on Wednesday. I used to run home from school, don my uniform, then trot to the lodge. The troop leader would lecture us on *die Weltanschauung*—the Party's outlook regarding Germany's role in the world. Our destiny was to wrest Europe from the clutches of Jewish finance, he told us. Very few of us believed that—we regarded it as a folktale for the provinces.

After class, we sang a Nazi medley whose purpose was to steel us for war. I can still feel my queasy stomach as I mouthed the words to Baumann's anthem: (Nowadays he pens children's books.)

The rotten bones of the world tremble
before war against the Reds,
We have broken the bonds of slavery
and head for a bigger triumph.
Everything shatters into glass,
as we continue our march;
For today Germany is ours and
tomorrow the whole world.

Through struggle, the world may crumble,
But as our debt to the devil comes due,
we'll build anew.
Everything shatters into glass,
as we continue our march;
For today Germany is ours and
tomorrow the whole world.

But the tunes weren't just truculent, they were ghoulish. Take for example our Flag Song, written by our leader Baldur von Schirach, whose American ancestors signed the Declaration of Independence:

Onward! Onward! Youth knows no danger…
Even though the bar is high,
youth still vaults it…
Our flag spells a new era: it leads us to eternity
—yes, it transcends death!

"Germany above Everything!" "The Flag Transcends Death!" This was nationalism at its most bizarre—statist theology.

On Saturdays we hiked to Köpenick Lake where, in warm weather, we swam, played soccer, and competed in races. Sundays were more serious: in the morning, *die Geländespiele* [terrain games]—military maneuvers for teenagers. Half of us would try to capture a hill, while the other half defended it. There were no weapons involved: each wore a string around his wrist—when it was torn, you were dead. In the afternoon, target practice—each would be handed a Mauser and a round of ammunition. Afterwards, we would crawl with these rifles, as if we were soldiers.

In June, some fifty troops from my district hiked to the Alps for a week of camping. We slept in barns, thanks to generous peasants. Many recall us trekking with tents in our packs, canteens over our shoulders, and compasses in our pockets. (The trick was to march without rattling the gear.) As we tramped, we sung *die Fahrtenlieder*—the dated hiking songs of *die Wandervögel* [the Roaming Birds], a nationalist youth movement at the turn of the century:

> Today we want to tie our backpacks,
> Pack them with carefree delight.
> Golden sun rays bring us joy,
> And the blackbird's call
> beckons us to the grove…

Once in the mountains, our days were again split: in the morning, we raced, jumped, and threw…earning "silver needles" for the quickest run, highest jump, and longest throw; by afternoon, it was time to *mut beweisen* [demonstrate courage]. Typically this was done by jumping from cliffs, although a platoon leader from Kassel once climbed a thirty-meter fir and leapt to a neighboring tree.

As night fell and sausages blackened, the demon returned: the infants of the Reich were again marking neighbors. Not every chorus was a Nazi one—the Kaiser had brewed his own storm. All around me were angelic faces lit by a trusting moon, munching wedged potatoes and sliced pickles. Crickets harmonized with the gushing stream, flames licked the wings of fireflies. It should have been paradise, this Alpine circle. But the Blitz was charted that night, London was scoped. Seemingly from nowhere, a cold rhyme welled from the nursery:

> Tonight we want to sing a wisp o' a tune
> We want to drink cool wine
> And the glasses should clink
> Then be pushed aside.
>
> Give me your hand, your white hand
> Farewell, my darling, farewell, farewell
> For we sail, for we sail
> For we sail against England.
>
> Our flag flying on the mast,
> Heralds the Reich's power,
> Which we will no longer bear
> The English laughing at.
> For we sail, for we sail
> For we sail against England. Ahoy!

1939 was a momentous year in my life. Hitler and Stalin signed their pact, which encouraged Germany to attack Poland, bringing Britain and France into the war. As part of the détente with the Soviets, many socialists and Communists were released from the camps—Mother was freed in October.

Earlier that year, I'd passed my *Abitur* and hoped to study philosophy with Heidegger in Freiburg. Mother never forgave him for having welcomed the regime, but by the late '30s he seemed more absorbed with Nietzsche than politics. Besides, he was the most brilliant mind in Germany.

But scholarship was impossible once the war began—'39 was the year of *die Musterung*, the Government's feverish draft registration. I either must join the Labor Service for six months and then the Wehrmacht as an enlistee…or enroll in war college to become an officer. The hour of the wolf had arrived—would Helga's son don a uniform in the service of National Socialism? I already wore the swastika as a member of *HJ*. But to spread fascism to Poland?

But what were my options? I could abandon Mother and try to emigrate, but to where? France, England, the U.S.? I doubted they wanted an *HJ*er, whose mother had been Red. Some of my friends were leaving for Russia, but after the Pact, what was the point? Hitler and Stalin were on the same team.

Fortunately, Mother was freed a week before enrollment. Within a day or two, she was advising me, but not in doctrinaire fashion. She'd become alienated from the Party after the Pact, and now considered herself a member of the "socialist community."

After dinner one evening, we all sat down to set my course—Martin and his pipe, Marie with her knitting, Mother and her shawl, and me. All eyes turned to Mother.

"National Socialism is Germany's monster," she began, "and must be destroyed by the world before it consumes it. Germans must play a role in this." Her gaze fixed on the curtains, those Silesian vineyards. "Friedrich will join the Wehrmacht as an officer. The Wehrmacht is German, not Nazi, and will inevitably turn against the regime."

"How can you be sure, Helga?" Marie challenged her.

Mother glared at her. "Because I cannot allow doubt any longer. The moment of decision has arrived, Marie. You must choose."

"Would you have the lad resist orders?"

"No, no, he fights bravely for the Reich." Her face stiffened. "Until that moment…"

2

They taught us to command at Wünsdorf—the hallowed art of bossing soldiers. As I completed my exams that first year, the Wehrmacht claimed Paris. In September, as the RAF stemmed the Luftwaffe, I was assigned to an *Abwehrschule* [military intelligence academy] for espionage training. It was located just outside Hamburg.

Abwehr was the intelligence section under the wartime Foreign Information and Counterintelligence Department. (The verb *abwehren* means to parry.) It traced its origins to the Intelligence Bureau begun by the Prussian General Staff in 1866. The bureau performed brilliantly in the Franco-Prussian War and World War I, but was retired for a few years after the Kaiser's abdication.

In 1921, the service was revived as the Abwehr under the direction of Colonel Gempp. The Nazis replaced Gempp in the early years of their rule. Their eventual choice, Captain (then Admiral) Wilhelm Canaris, would become one of their opponents. Yet even while garnering vital intelligence in the late '30s, Canaris maintained autonomy from the Gestapo and *SD* (Security Service).

During the war, the Abwehr would become a beehive of resistance to National Socialism. Lutheran philosopher Dietrich Bonhoeffer would betray the regime under

15

Abwehr protection. And many Abwehr officers—including Canaris and his deputy, Oster—would conspire against Hitler. In early '44, the agency was abolished.

How did *der* Dassen fit into this puzzle? The Wehrmacht wanted me to become an expert on energy—specifically, the network through which the Commonwealth obtained oil. By graduation, they'd decided to move me to Tripoli to conjure ways of disrupting delivery. But the endgame was to place me in Europe to assist an embargo.

By the '40s, there were dozens of *Abwehrschulen* throughout the Reich. Obviously they weren't Nazi… but what they lacked in ideology, they balanced with cunning. These were some of the most insidious academies in the history of warfare. Inside their warrens, the ore of social science was pitilessly smelt by imperial lust. And the result was heavy metal:

"The British Empire," *Herr Dozent* [Instructor] Kleist shouted the first week of the term, "is not a thing." He pounded on the lectern. "*Nein, meine Herren*, it is not an object like this lectern. IT IS A CONCEPT! AN IDEA! *IHR FEIND* [YOUR ENEMY]!"

Fritz Kleist was something of a madman that fall, with wild black hair brushing against his tunic. But at twenty-five, he was a lauded historian and eclectic theorist. And his class, "The Mystique of Empire," anticipated Fanon by more than a decade.

He pointed to Australia on the globe. "What impels her mines to ship their opals to Britain? Is it the market? *Nein*, prices are higher in New York. It is loyalty! Loyalty to the Mother Country, which suckled the colony in the previous century. Loyalty to the Anglo-Saxon race that impels Britain, Canada, Australia, and New Zealand…but which may be sullied in America. Loyalty to Anglo-Saxon culture that defines Britain, Canada, Australia, and New Zealand…but which may be sullied in America. Loyalty to Anglican Christianity…which may be diluted in America. Loyalty to parliamentary democracy, whose community, it is granted, encompasses more than Britain, Canada, Australia, and New Zealand—it is thought to include America, France, and Scandinavia as well. And finally, yes, loyalty to the Crown, which has traditionally reigned over the English people."

Although Kleist considered himself a nationalist, his analysis of empire betrayed a Marxian perspective. It was a synthesis of Marx' theory of "superstructure"… with Lenin's notion of imperialism…with (Italian Marxist) Gramsci's concept of ideological "hegemony." For Kleist, British power surely rested on commercial capitalism. But the dynamic of that capitalism—the *soul* of its domination—was sustained through "mystification."

The *dozent* paced the floor. "If these sentimental ties," he warned, "this shared nostalgia between America and the Empire cannot be weakened, the prospects for Germany are bleak. The Reich cannot alone rely on military technology. That will only take it so far—it will not triumph in this manner. Its mission must be to fragment the Empire at every level—economics, race, history, culture, spirit, politics."

Kleist identified with the wave of populism that had

17

transformed German academia. During Weimar, for example, it was rare for a *dozent* to accompany students to the *Mensa* [cafeteria]. But on several occasions, Kleist did just that. "If candidates are eager to wrestle with ideas while they dine," he told the dean, "I am willing to guide them. This war will not be won with morning lectures but evening billiards."

One evening in November, Kleist joined me and two colleagues—Otto Frisch, an aristocrat from Leipzig, and Helmut Wolff, whose father was a Frankfurt attorney. Wolff was skeptical about Kleist's approach. "Here is the nub of my confusion, *Herr Dozent*," he explained, as he sipped his stein. "You say the Anglos are wedded to their culture. Fine. But how can the Reich hope to sever this bond? 'What God hath joined, let no man put asunder.'"

The instructor lit a cigarette. "The precise way any marriage is dissolved, Wolff—by divorce." He smiled.

"But what should the Ministry tell the English—Goethe trumps Shakespeare?"

Kleist warmed to the challenge. "*Nein*, no criticism of Shakespeare—that is sacred ground." We chuckled. "But music, philosophy…What is their music? Purcell? Handel and Hayden in London? Can this compare with Bach, Mozart, Beethoven, Wagner, Brahms? Philosophy—who do they have? Hume? Can he compare with Kant, Hegel, Nietzsche?"

But Wolff kept smiling. "But, *Herr Dozent*, how do you apply this? Do you drop *Zarathustra* over London?"

The *dozent* flicked his ashes. "No, of course not. Their

intelligentsia must be engaged. They must be weaned from their Bentham."

"But a war is on, *Herr Dozent*!" Frisch interjected. "A struggle!"

"*Ja*, and I don't know if this mania is in the Reich's interest."

Frisch emptied the pitcher into his stein. "You think perhaps there should be a period of consolidation…during which the Reich should attempt to sever the loyalty of English-speaking people to the Empire?"

The *dozent* chose his words. "Such a contest has been transpiring since Bach."

I stood up—it was time to unmask the charade. "But, *Herr Dozent*, what you are proposing is peace!" Wolff giggled.

Kleist smiled, then snuffed his cigarette. "*Nein*, Dassen," he sighed, "there can no longer be peace. Buckingham has been strafed—blood has been drawn. They will not rest until Berlin is shambles—I know their taste for retribution." He pulled up closer to the table and lowered his voice. "What is best for the Reich is an extended period of combat—perhaps a decade or more…*ja*…at times military, at times cultural, at times diplomatic." He lit a match and let it falter. "War at a low flame, *meine Herren*."

Frisch had expressed similar thoughts, but played devil's advocate that night. "*Blitzkrieg* has acquitted itself quite well, *Herr Dozent*—Poland, Belgium, France…"

The instructor was sarcastic. "Oh *ja*, Poland, Belgium, France. But Stalin's still here, Roosevelt's here…and I'm beginning to fear, *meine Herren*, that after the dust settles, Churchill will be here also." We smiled. Then he protected himself: "But we are speaking prospectively, of course; this is merely strategic evaluation. We are grateful to *der Führer* for having revived the challenge to the Empire…for having made resistance possible."

"*Jawohl!*", we chorused, like old men in the rear of a church.

♦

There were attractive women on the grounds, most of whom were assigned to the Project in the rear of campus. (The effort entailed the analysis of data from the Middle East.) When I arrived, my fellow candidates were dating these women. But one of them, a statistician named Ursula, had declined invitations.

It was while playing Ping-Pong on Christmas that Otto broke the news. "You know, *Kumpel*, Ursula is intrigued by you," he told me while retrieving the ball. "You should invite her to the Saturday movie."

His serve clipped the table—I returned it with a backhand. "Which one is she?"

He caught the ball and pointed at me. "Wake up, *junge*. You live in a trance."

I smiled. "Was she the one at the cafe?"

"*Ja!*" he shouted impatiently, "the blonde from Stuttgart!" He cued my memory. "The statistician?…Her beau died in Poland?…"

I nodded. "Oh, *ja*. But she seemed more interested in you."

"Because you wouldn't talk to her! You were gazing at airplanes!" I shrugged. "Do yourself a favor, Friedrich—ask her to *Ballnacht* [Cotillion]. It's a good film."

But I despised the director. "Froelich, that toady. I hated *Heimat* [Homeland]."

"*Ballnacht* is better. No patriotism."

His serve was shallow and I lunged for it; then managed a weak return that was smashed past me. "How do you know she's intrigued?" I called out, as I snatched the ball from the couch.

He moved two fingers like a beak. "A little bird, a tiny little bird."

♦

"Have you ever gone with a wealthy woman?" she asked in the candlelight. The music was Bach; the coffee, Turkish. *Ballnacht* had limned a romance between a composer and society belle.

I felt I could trust her. "There were difficulties in my family. I haven't gone out much at all."

She nodded. "Of course." It was rare for women to wear their hair down during the war but she did so that night—bright yellow strands halfway down her sweater. And a swaying quality to her body, as if she were about to become a butterfly. A fugue swelled on the gramophone. "To be honest, Friedrich, growing up in the Black

21

Forest, I never conceived of this world—the tanks, the planes, Poland, France. Even Hitler seemed…"

"You saw him as a father? Guarding the firs?" There was a trace of bitterness in my voice.

"I never thought of him as *Kriegsherr* [war captain]. I was only a girl then."

I was divided in my feelings. On one hand, it would have been easy to walk to the hotel and in the attic room overlooking the tower possess this woman once, twice, into the night. One would hardly have known the reason, except the thrill.

But the fact is I was barely sexual in Germany. There was something about the regimentation that depressed me. The rallies, the speakers—they offended me. I longed for the Alpine cabin, the swim in the stream, the campus seminar, the Quartet in G. Yes, Mozart, live on the lakefront, with fishing boats fading in the sky.

"*Ein herrlicher Entschluß* [Superb resolution]!" I'd congratulate the cellist, with my arm around my daughter and my pipe in my pocket.

The bow would be deep. "*Es war uns ein Vergnügen, mein Herr* [Our pleasure, sir]."

But sex? It seemed too large a donation. How could one bestow passion inside this reformatory? Ennui overtook me and, from Ursula's perch, a vacant scowl was noted, a gesture of detachment.

And what was returned was this eulogy of Heinz—the fallen beau, the bronze captain of the 4th Panzer. I was compelled to partake of a vicarious tableau—either that, or carnal identification with the woman before me. And

22

this *cosi simpatico*, this transmigration, seemed to be demanded as penance for rejecting her.

For in her reverie was this synthesis—this Nazi collage—of the muscled body in Stuttgart, writhing under her Daddy's sheets (while Papa wintered in Palma), with a bare-chested platoon hacking dazed youths to death. Yes, some sort of chaos, where Aryan and Slav wrestled *mano-à-mano* on the arid steppe. And in the end, a slaughter of Poles and six Iron Crosses, posthumously given.

She stared at the gramophone. "I wish I had borne his child. We were waiting until after the war."

I sipped my cappuccino. "There are other men."

She winced. "I suppose so," she agreed. But was disgusted with me.

♦

The last time I saw Kleist was in a seedy bar by the wharf. He hadn't shaved in days and was nursing a bottle of vodka. I'd been visiting my uncle's shop and had stopped by for a Riesling.

I ordered my glass and joined him at his table. A polka played on the radio. "I have given my resignation, Dassen," he told me. "The course will be completed by Scheuler."

"Why?" I wondered.

He shrugged his shoulders. "The dean required it. 'Defeatism'."

23

"Defeatism? But you're completely loyal to the Reich!"

He refilled his glass. "Twenty thousand civilians dead in Belgrade! On Easter Sunday no less! For what?" He searched my eyes. "For what reason?"

"The coup, the king..." I mumbled.

He threw up his hands. "France, Poland—even Norway—one understands this. These are contenders. But Yugoslavia? This is pure adventure—conquest for the sake of it." He raised his voice in indignation. "No ideology, no rationale"—his jaw clenched—"just dumb, *hitzig* [hot-headed] Hitler!"

The situation was becoming dangerous—the *dozent* was drunk and caviling *der Führer*. It's true the bar was empty, and this was Hamburg not Berlin, but one couldn't trust the bartender, old as he was. I glared at Kleist coldly. "Try to be discreet. For my sake, if not yours."

"*Jawohl*," he muttered. I took a breath. He lowered his voice. "Why do you remain here? You have connections. You could be in Sweden tomorrow."

I sipped my wine nervously. "What are you talking about?" I whispered. "I have no connections."

"But you do," he insisted. "You're looking at one."

Although Kleist undoubtedly had friends, I had no idea how subversive they were...or would become. At that moment, I simply couldn't trust his clique to smuggle me to Sweden or support me once I was there. Besides, Mother had charted my mission.

"Are you emigrating?" I whispered. He nodded. I shook my head. "*Nein*, this is not for me."

"You will serve *der Kriegsherr?*"

"Men of honor must remain in the Wehrmacht," I explained. Our eyes locked. *"Bewachen von innen* [To guard from within]…"

3

I graduated in June '41, and was dispatched to Tripoli as first lieutenant. Just after my arrival, *Die Dune*—the weekly newspaper of the Afrika Korps—greeted me as one of the "promising new graduates from Wünsdorf." My photo reveals a rookie in khaki sporting the tropical armband—swastika *cum* palm tree. A silver eagle crests my cap. I was nearly six feet tall. And innocent.

They planned to use me in Paris after a stint in Libya, but like nearly everything else that befell them, history did not cooperate. A year later, Montgomery routed Rommel in Egypt, and the Korps regrouped in Tunis. Yet the Tunisian site was no more secure: after landing in Algeria in late '42, Ike rushed to meet Monty, and by May we were his prisoners. They took 130,000 Germans, over 100,000 Italians.

Prisoner of War—the thought had never occurred to me. I'd been so anxious about the dilemma of shooting Russians, I never conceived spending the war in a camp. And where would I be held? In the Sahara? England?

Our unit was tossed on a flatcar and sent to Morocco. Upon arrival, officers were culled from the barbed pen where some 50,000 men baked in the sun. Instead, we

27

were stuffed into bunkers.

The next morning we were quizzed by the Yanks. There'd been rumors of spooks being shot for recalcitrance so you wanted to at least make conversation. Fortunately, my interrogator showed little interest in me.

We awaited him on a bench outside his trailer. I was the first summoned. An assistant came out to fetch me. "Lieutenant Dah-sen?" he asked hesitantly. I stood and saluted. "Corporal Mulligan will see you now."

My inquisitor was buried in a file and didn't acknowledge my salute. He was short and angular, with a flushed face. I sat on a chair in front of his table, while a clerk scribbled behind me.

The corporal reviewed my form. "Analyst, 17th…" Then looked up. "What do you analyze, Lieutenant?" There was a touch of sarcasm in his voice. But it worked in my favor.

"Fuel, Corporal: petrol, water…" There were photos of FDR and Churchill on the wall—welcome to Allied Van Lines.

"Yours or ours?"

"Yours."

"Oh, yeah? Well, whaddya think, Lieutenant, we got enough oil?"

I smiled. "It is appearing so, Corporal."

"Did the Abwehr send you on trips—Arabia, the Gulf?"

"No, Corporal."

"No missions, eh?" He stamped my form. "Very well, Lieutenant. You'll have some time to practice your

English now."

"Shall we go to England, Corporal?"

"Who's asking the questions here?" he retorted with a smirk. He placed my form in the file. "Hasn't been decided, Lieutenant. Check with your CO on Friday."

But news came sooner. The following evening an American major noticed me and Captain Raubel in the officer's mess. "What's the matter, Lieutenant? You look nervous."

I was actually concerned about Mother, who in a coded letter implied she might join the Underground. But I covered for myself. "We worry of where we go, Major."

"Don't want to pay a visit to Uncle Joe, eh?"

I smiled. "No, Major."

He stamped his foot on the bench. "Well, you fellas can just relax. Because y'all're headin' for the U S of A."

I couldn't believe it. "Major, you are joking us."

"Not a chance, Lieutenant. All POWs here are shipping for the States next week."

I wanted to hug him—I couldn't believe my luck. For the rest of the war, I'd be out of Europe, out of the desert…SAFE! "Oh, this is very good news, Major!"

"All right, then, officers." He rose to go, then waved a finger at me. "Now, y'all work hard for Uncle Sam. You know, they're puttin' your boys in the fields out West."

"The *fields*, Major?"

"Yup, German field hands—can you beat that?" He slapped his thigh. "Now y'all do a good job."

I was about to assure him we would, then caught

myself—after all, the Swiss might object to such assignment.

That night I lay awake thinking about Russia—what if I'd been sent there? As an officer from a Communist family, how would I've been treated? Would the Russians have given me a platoon? In high school, I'd led the false life of an *HJ*er; in Tunis, the false life of an agent. I had no politics—I couldn't afford them. So how would I have proven myself?

"My Mother's in the Underground."

"Why aren't you with her, comrade?" they might ask.

4

How to continue without reviewing the facts?

Between '39 and '45, Germany killed over 15 million enemy soldiers and wounded over 7 million. It murdered over 17 million civilians, including 6 million Russians, 5 million Jews, 3 million Poles, and a half million Gypsies. Some of these civilians died in bombings and sieges, but most were either shot in villages, gassed in vans, or starved, exhausted, shot, or gassed in camps. Among those "cleansed" were some 15,000 homosexuals.

It was a German illness and a human illness.

It was a German illness because for the sixty-odd years before Hitler's accession, Germany failed to embrace liberalism as had England, France, and Scandinavia. The Second Reich nurtured contempt for democracy and pluralism...and respect for authority and war. And it seemed to do so without offending national conscience: key prelates and intellectuals (Hegel, Treitschke) came to rationalize the authoritarian state—Treitschke, in fact, endorsing expansion, racism, antisemitism.

But it was a human illness as well. For after the people lost God, power, wealth, and hope, what did they have in '30? Only the vacant stars mocking them at night.

I sit here in my seventies overlooking the Golden

Gate, a retired professor. Loyalty to my mother spared me from fascism. Africa excused me from the Eastern front. The Allied victory catapulted me to democracy. After receiving citizenship, I've consistently voted for every liberal I could find—Stevenson, Carter, Mondale, Dukakis. I want peace and quiet, the middle of the river, a humble exit.

I contemplate Germany's spree, and sink into the abyss. Suddenly the fog that descended on *Deutschland* engulfs me as well. I cannot help it: evil—even its memory—is stronger than my will.

I am murderer and victim. I will be nauseous and ashamed when I recover. But you will help me recover. You will quote some shrink saying there's a void in us all, and given proper circumstance, may corrode each of us.

I sink deeper. I can feel the sadistic thrill of turning the valve—I masturbate with a huge erection on the metal handle.

Suddenly I'm a victim in a Polish pit. They have shot me in the leg, but I'm still alive. I fuck a nun against her will—it's painful for her. I press her into a teenager bleeding from the elbow. The SS is offended and shoots my buttocks off. I die a sacrilegious rapist, as morally depraved as my captors. I die giving away the one thing I might have withheld.

I'm a newly-arrived officer at Auschwitz, living in a cottage with flower beds. Soon after arriving, I realize National Socialism is a smoke screen for genocide. But the pension plan is excellent.

The gramophone plays Beethoven's Violin Concerto

and I dream of deserting. Lift me, reader.

But I cannot entirely trust Beethoven. *Es muss sein* may be more than personal resignation—it may be our death sentence. Lift me, reader.

But I cannot entirely trust Goethe. His redemption of Faust may validate Western madness. Lift me, reader.

Ah, but I can trust the Jitterbug the Americans dance. Or the cigar Groucho smokes.

All right, then, sail on. Let the tale continue.

5

It's unusual for a visitor to glimpse the U.S. ten leagues from Norfolk, but that's how I first saw it. The approach began with the sighting of a lighthouse, then beyond that restless beam into the open Chesapeake. Then a graze by Fort Monroe with its towering flagpole, before crossing Hampton Roads into the floodlit Navy yard. As we docked, a B-24 pierced the sky.

"*Mein Gott!*" gasped the corporal next to me, "do they not know it is war?"

"Very bright here, eh Corporal?"

"The city, the wharf—lights everywhere!" He rubbed his eyes. "I am not believing this!"

Years later my students wondered about the dangers of crossing the ocean during wartime. But it was perfectly safe, because the Germans were respecting POW ships, providing they flew the Red Cross and sailed with their lights on.

The Navy deloused us after we disembarked—burned our uniforms, sprayed our bodies, issued us outfits. Afterwards we queued for orders. I can still remember the smile on the WAC's face as she tucked my papers in the envelope. "Well, Lieutenant, looks like you and the captain are off to Teton."

"*Tee*-tohn?" I struggled. "Let me look please at *meine Karte*."

I fumbled with the map as she pointed to a square in the West. Now it was my turn to gasp. "*Mein Gott*, this is far!"

"Yep, big country we got here, Lieutenant. You'll ride four days before you get to Carson."

I found Carson, then pointed to it. "And the camp is just there?"

She ran her finger north. "Well, no, upstate…past Antelope…over here by Split Creek…see it? The coach'll take you to Carson—then they'll bus you boys up."

"Coach" was right. Instead of the boxcars the Wehrmacht carted us around in, the Americans sent us in Pullmans with porters. Our sergeants hesitated to lead their squads in, certain the cars were for officers only.

En route, my comrades suffered another surprise— many believed Goebbels' lie about widespread damage inflicted by the Luftwaffe. But as we sped through Ohio, it was clear the U.S. was vast and untouched, with an army of trains and trucks attending extensive industry.

My God, what a Goliath Adolf had roused! I kept thinking of his speech just before the war: "Mr. Roosevelt, I fully comprehend the vastness of your nation and immense wealth of your country. Alas, I am placed in a more modest sphere." *Ja*, Adolf: it's called Losing.

As we approached the capital, a lame joke was cracked: "Ah, Columbus!" shouted a wag. "This is where the Spaniard lands!" I turned around to correct the prankster. "*Nein*, Corporal, it was the Caribbean. And he was

Italian." "Oh, the Axis!" the wag shot back, amid general laughter.

We were in Nebraska the third day. The diehards were still saying America couldn't be intact—the train had to be going in circles. I assured the sergeant beside me we were proceeding directly.

"*Ja*, it's a poor country just the same," he baited me.

"Sergeant, are you blind?" I snapped, pointing out the window. "Even in the countryside, there are autos and lorries wherever you look."

"*Ja*, Lieutenant, but few stone houses."

It was summer in the Midwest and, by afternoon, the coaches were warm. We couldn't fully open the windows because the Army had nailed planks over them. But because there were officers in our car, the guards relented and removed the boards. My first taste of Yankee kindness.

After dinner Captain Raubel and I were introduced to science fiction. One of the porters gave us some issues of *Amazing*—"You boys need to scope dem *other* worlds!" he teased. "Looks like you done blooown your gig in dis one!" His partners guffawed in the rear. Aficionados will recall that five years earlier John Campbell revitalized the monthly, nurturing a fresh crew of storytellers, such as Asimov, Van Vogt, Bradbury, and Heinlein.

On the bus upstate, we spied Bent Arrow—the foothills of the Rockies. For the first time since Mother and I hiked the Alps, I felt topographic excitement. How can one explain the thrill of the West? For a European dodging the martial flame, it was a brisk shower—the cut of the peaks, the gale off the snow, the lurid sky. Ah, Teton—I came Nazi, I left free.

♦

The commandant of Camp Roberts met us at the gate. His name was Captain Collins, and he looked like Jimmy Stewart. He stood on a makeshift platform and surveyed the newcomers, while a half dozen riflemen scoped us from the rooftops. As he spoke, his German assistant, Captain Rausch, intermittently translated:

> Officers, soldiers: You've lost a campaign, your nation will lose this war, yet you yourselves are fortunate. You've been liberated from a tyranny and shipped to a free land. Here, you are safe to doubt—as Americans have always doubted—the prudence of dictatorship and the morality of subjugation.

> Towards this end, you will all be decently housed and fed. Soldiers will be required to earn their keep. Officers—we'll assist you in pursuits of your choice.

> Detail will commence Monday at 0700 hours. Once you're settled, Captain Rausch will communicate my orders to the designated officer or sergeant of each compound.

> On behalf of your Captain, my staff, and myself, I'd like to extend a summer greeting to you all: *Willkommen in Teton! Willkommen in America!*

Camp Roberts had cost Uncle Sam $800,000. It contained three compounds whose units were linked by gravel lanes—a camp for NCOs and enlistees north of

38

the highway, an adjoining recreational compound, and an officers camp across the road. By summer, there'd be 125,000 German soldiers in the U.S—by mid-'45, over 350,000 housed in 150 base camps in the rural West, Plains, Great Lakes, and South. Roberts housed 2200.

North Camp boasted nearly fifty cabins, fifteen by fifty feet, each with twenty double-decker bunks and a pot-belly stove. Cabins were concrete with tar roofs and pine interiors. There were five mess halls and nine latrines. More importantly, the showers were hot.

Our sergeants were stunned by the luxury. In Africa, they were lucky if there was enough straw for their squads. Here each prisoner enjoyed a mattress on a spring, two sheets, an encased pillow, and a cotton blanket. And ate with silverware on porcelain plates.

The "Rec" consisted of nearly a dozen structures—an infirmary/clinic, library, chapel, post office, PX/canteen, laundry, theater, mechanics/wood shop, gym, and warehouse. Around its perimeter were a soccer field, tennis court, volleyball court—later, a vegetable garden.

Activities were numerous. In addition to sports, reading, and correspondence, there was a theater troupe, chorus, orchestra, jazz band, easels, box games, chess sets, playing cards…even a kennel to house exotic pets like parrots and monkeys.

In South Camp across the road, some 200 junior officers shared six-room cottages, each with its own common room and five bedrooms. Senior officers had been sent to Mississippi.

Yet the camp was still prison. It was encircled by a

pair of ten-foot fences placed eight feet apart. Fifty-foot towers, each with searchlight and machine gun, squared each corner. Yet compared to Russia, Roberts was a godsend. A captain once joked to me that if he'd known about the camp, "I would have told Rommel to surrender. *Von vornherein!* [From the outset!]"

♦

On the third morning, Rausch summoned me. He wasn't much older than I was, and considerably stockier. I saluted him conventionally—the Wehrmacht discouraged the Hitler arm until Berlin imposed it the following summer.

He motioned me to sit down, then ruffled through my file. He pulled no punches: "Your mother was a Communist, Lieutenant?"

Had she been caught? What did they know? "In the '20s, Captain."

He kept ruffling. "*Ja*, my uncle as well—socialist—don't worry about it." He spoke matter-of-factly. I muffled a sigh.

He rushed through the report. "'Protective custody, Sachsenhausen. Living in Berlin, apparel designer. No current activity...'" A second heave.

He looked up. "And *your* politics, Lieutenant?"

"None, Captain."

He smiled. "Good. This war can't last much longer. The Allies are already in Italy." Through his window, I

40

could see a heifer across the road, chewing cud in the shadow…and the snow-capped Antlers scraping the horizon. He coughed. "Well, your secret is safe with me, Lieutenant. I have no desire to cause you discomfort." I nodded. "But you should know there's a group of fanatics here—well, nearly every camp really. You know, *Großen Tiere* [big shots] set on purging 'unpatriotic' elements." He shrugged an apology.

"But the Americans—"

He waved his hand. "*Ja*, the Americans have taken a liking towards these zealots. They've handed many of the camps over to them."

"But, Captain…why?"

He threw up his hands and smiled. "No one knows really. Some of the commandants admire their ability to accomplish things. How do they put it?—'deliver the goods.'"

"What goods, Captain?"

He leaned forward; his body was tense. "Lieutenant, the Americans have put our men to work."

"Yes, Captain, I have heard this."

There was a long silence—he restlessly shuffled the papers on his desk. "PRODUCTION, DASSEN!" he exploded. He shouted it as if it were the century's curse word. "ASSISTING THE WAR EFFORT! *VERSTEHEN SIE?*"

"Yes, Captain, I am understanding."

"Good! Glad you got it!" He was sick of the war.

I took a breath. "What here is the situation, Captain? Who is running the camp?"

He tapped his pencil. "Too early to tell, Lieutenant.

41

Really couldn't say." He rose, and I quickly met him. "I may rely on your discretion, Lieutenant."

"Of course, Captain."

He looked down. "I suppose you heard the Commandant permits officers to travel about—well, within 50 miles of camp. This depends, of course, on your assurance."

"You have my word, Captain." (As if one would willingly leave! And run where?—Rostov?)

He faced me. "Good, Lieutenant. You will initially be assigned a guard. But after you learn the land, I see no reason…"

I met his eyes. "I appreciate your confidence, Captain." He nodded. I saluted, then turned to go, but curiosity welled. "Captain, forgive me, but is your uncle well?"

He'd returned to his papers. "No, I am afraid not."

I bowed my head. "I am sorry."

He didn't look up. "*Ja*, they beat him to death."

♦

Later that week, Rausch ordered me to observe a team on detail, whose task was to thin beets on a farm down the road: "Officers are not participating in these projects," he explained, "but you seem like a sensible fellow and, er"—he leafed through a booklet—"I may have occasion to ask your assistance."

"How shall I help, Captain?"

He looked me in the eye. "By mediating, Lieutenant."

"What is *mee*-dee-ating, Captain?"

"Die Vermittlung," he barked.

"Ach so! With the Americans, Captain?"

He shook his head. *"Nein,* disputes between our own men."

I was flattered. "This is—how does *man* say?—the privilege, Captain." I bowed.

He nodded. "Very well, Lieutenant. Tomorrow you report to Corporal Larsen. Just before 0800 hours. You will go out with a team. I want you to get, er, a flavor..." His voice trailed off as he scanned a page.

"A 'flavor,' Captain?"

He waved his hand, still reading. *"Ja,* the way they are living..."

The following morning, there were some twenty pickups in the parking lot, each with a number taped to its windshield. I found Corporal Beck at the end of the row—a muscular NCO with oiled black hair. He introduced me to the driver, a local farmboy named Dave, and Private Evans, the U.S. guard. Dave shook my hand, Evans saluted. "The Lieutenant is today in the front riding," Beck told the guard. Then motioned Evans and a dozen men to board the truck bed before joining them.

That morning in the farmhouse, I chatted with Evans and Eve Koch, the farmer's wife. Mrs. Koch was boiling soup in the kitchen. Evans had stood his rifle in the corner and stacked a pile of comics on the table.

I turned to him. "You must watch the prisoners in the field?"

He and Eve laughed. "Don't worry," he grinned,

"those boys ain't goin' nowhere." He pointed to his weapon. "Hell, some days I *give* 'em the damn gun... y'know, for rabbits."

Eve pointed out the window. "A man would be crazy to run for the hills, Lieutenant. In summer?" She cupped her mouth. "My Lord, they'd starve!...Here, they can have my soup, a concert, and an afternoon swim."

Concert? Swim? I looked over to Evans but he was deep into Archie as the sky rumbled and rain filled the gutters.

To my amazement, lunch was served in the dining room that morning. Eve's husband Pete offered an explanation, as he hung his poncho on a hook: "When it's squallin' like this, there's no reason to drench 'em. That's my philosophy."

"They are not eating the lunch from their sacks?"

He rolled up his sleeves. "Lieutenant, what the camp gives 'em is a piece of white bread, a slice of salami, and an apple." He waved his finger at me. "That's not enough to sustain a man." He pointed to the stockpot. "Your corporal came over to chew me out about this last month. I told him, 'Corporal, if I can't feed 'em, take 'em back. Anybody's workin' for me, I'm not havin 'im pass out in my field. This ain't no slave camp.'" He pointed to his plate. "They get a bowl of soup, a wedge of *real* bread, and I get a day's work." He nodded sharply.

After lunch, a young sergeant played Chopin on an old upright while the men sipped Folger's. After a nocturne, Pete motioned me out to the porch. "I wanna show you our new shop, Lieutenant." Then walked me across the lawn to a small cabin. Inside were lumber, tools, and an electric saw and drill. "What with the shortages, the farms can't get house furniture. But babies are being born in this valley." He pointed to the saw. "So come winter, we'll be carvin' right here. Should bring in some extra change."

"*Wunderbar!*" I smiled.

He dusted the blade, then looked up. "So, Lieutenant, what's yer take on this Hitler feller?"

I'd expected some politics. "You are German from before?"

He nodded. "Oh, yeah. Papa left Essen before the First One. Eve's folks have been here forever."

"You like America?"

He raised his hands and grinned. "Look around you!"

I cupped my mouth with my hand: "I think Hitler is biting more than he eats." Then giggled.

He slapped my back. "More than he can chew—my thoughts exactly! You don't take on the Brits, the Bear, and the Yanks in one swoop!" Then shook his head. "What a lunatic!"

Just after five, Dave drove us back to camp, while the men sang "Row Your Boat" in harmony. "Damn, they're good!" Dave squealed, as we passed a milk truck. "They oughtta go down to Carson and play the Palace!"

But I changed the subject. "Dave, say me, please…the farmers are happy with our POWs?"

The lad nodded. "Oh, sure, Lieutenant." He pointed behind him. "These guys run circles around the wetbacks. No comparison."

"No trouble?" I probed.

"No, sir…Well, I mean, last month Dad got cross with a few of 'em." He grinned. "You know, some of 'em wanted to ride Aces or take the truck for a spin."

"'Aces' is your horse?"

Dave checked his mirror. "Our saddle horse, yeah."

"But that is all the problem—with the horse?"

We pulled into the parking lot. Dave pulled the handbrake and looked me in the eye. "Lieutenant, these guys are the best we've ever had. No one likes this War, but we'll all be sorry to see 'em go. And that's the damn truth."

◆

I wasn't as sure as Rausch the war would end quickly. Hitler still held Europe from Rome to Oslo, from Smolensk to the Pyrenees. It could all take several years—I could rot here in Teton. I had to find something to do.

I decided to deliver Heidegger from his pessimism. In *Being & Time*, he'd sounded totally desperate. Humanity is hopelessly trapped in "facticity," he'd complained— doomed to *das Herstellbare*, the compulsive collection of gadgets. Radios, automobiles, airplanes merely contribute to the Darkening of the World. In this material dusk, humanity becomes *unheimlich* [estranged from its core], and each is left to dread his death.

For Kierkegaard, the way out of materialism was the

leap into faith. But Heidegger is a child of Nietzsche and God is out of the question. He prefers the pre-Socratic concept of *Seiend*—a holistic notion of Being that predates logic.

But he never defines it—only dances around it. For the individual, *Seiend* is the *eigentlich* [authentic] persona located in *der Grund* [the Ground] of the Self. It's reached via *die Spur des Heiligen*—the Whiff of the Sacred. Though it can't be captured, it must be realized. Conscience demands that we arrest our *Verfallen* [surrender] to facticity and reclaim our essence.

My effort to rescue Heidegger from despair seemed a worthy task. Both American consumerism and Soviet Marxism seemed doomed to disappoint—humanity couldn't subsist on collective farms or RCA. There had to be a dynamic greater than progress.

But what was it? That was the problem I faced in the mountains: could inspiration brave the death of God?

To be sure, nothing so solicitous would be tolerated back home. But that's precisely why Heidegger was desperate! With imagination confined, no one could rescue him!

Yet here on the buttes, the fitful wind doubts everything—the Past is always in question. As in Rilke:

Ein Hauch um nichts. Ein Wehn im Gott.
Ein Wind.
[A breath around nothing. A pang within God.
A breeze.]

◆

The librarian in Shelburne, the pudgy wife of a banker, visited every Friday to obtain and fulfill requests. Scholarly and German titles were retrieved by her library, which sent a van every week to the university downstate. Mrs. Cotler would then deliver the books to camp.

She brightened when I asked for *Process and Reality*. "What a wonderful choice, Lieutenant! Are you a student of philosophy?" I nodded bashfully. "Oh my," she teased, "a handsome lieutenant and a scholar too. No wonder they keep you locked up!"

I blushed. She reached for her pile. "You're permitted off-premises, Lieutenant?"

"Usually, *ja*. With an escort."

"Ah yes, officer's code—what a splendid tradition." She added a book to her stack, then looked up. "Well, I wonder if you'd care to join our group at Professor Bates' ranch. We're discussing Nietzsche's *Beyond Good and Evil* this week. Tim used to teach at UT."

"This is the Teton University?" I asked. She nodded. "But where is the ranch, Mrs. Cotler?"

She pointed towards the hills. "Just up the road. In Pennant."

I shook my head. "*Ja*, but Pennant is already near Shelburne—"

She waved her hand. "Oh, don't worry about that. Nancy Pell drives up from Antelope. I'll have her give you a lift. She can be your escort."

She proved to be a schoolteacher with an immaculate Ford. The Ink Spots crackled on her radio. But the engine smelled strange.

"Is that petrol?" I asked.

She laughed. "No one in the valley runs on gas anymore, Lieutenant. Four gallons a week barely gets you to the grocery."

"*Ach so*, the rationing."

"'*Ach so*, the rationing,'" she mimicked. Then pointed to the hood. "That's kerosene in there."

"Kerosene?"

She nodded. "We start the car with gas, then fill it with kerosene."

"And they are not rationing this?"

She shook our head. "Why, no, Lieutenant, there's plenty of *that!*" The music switched to Dorsey and she changed the subject. "So tell me, are you boys comfortable at camp?"

I cracked my window. "Oh, yes, Miss Pell, we are certainly. The American camps by far beat any other. We are here eating better than in the Wehrmacht."

She smiled wryly. "Yes, some folks in town think Uncle Sam is coddling you boys. One of them calls your place the 'Fritz Ritz'!"

"Fritz, this is meaning a German person?" She nodded. "And Ritz?"

"Ritz is…well, like a luxury hotel—like the Ritz Carlton." The beam of a truck lit her hairpin.

I sighed. "*Ja*, one of my mates is calling camp *Der Goldene Käfig*. Are you speaking German, Miss Pell?"

"*Käfig, Käfig...*" She bit her lip. "Uh, the Golden Cage?"

"Right-o!" I laughed, trying out some slang.

She chuckled, then downshifted as we climbed a hill. Then more seriously: "I'm not opposed to the camps being decent. It said in the *Eagle* last week that word's gettin' round that our camps are tolerable—I mean, among Germans at the front. It seems to me that could lighten resistance…"

♦

Bates' ranch wallowed in foothill charm. The bay window framed the Antlers, while the fireplace rose to the ceiling. In the dining room, a dozen of us huddled around his oak table.

His analysis of Nietzsche was harmless enough: he correctly noted the philosopher's alienation from Christian ethics. It was only toward the end of the evening I became suspicious of my new friends.

The ringleader was a rancher named Bud Hoffman, whose parents had apparently been Sudeten. Bald, husky, bronzed, Hoffman was physically intimidating yet intellectually sharp. He was the sort of man who aroused dread by the languor with which he returned a stein to the table…and the speed with which he retrieved it. (Oh Bud, if only you'd stood defeat!)

"The essential point," Bates concluded as his daughter filled the nut tray, "is that for Nietzsche the 'revaluation of values' refuses Christianity."

Hoffman filled his stein—the head rose to the brim. Then shook his head. "I don't think that's it, Tim."

There was a silence. "You don't think he's rejecting Christ?"

"Oh he's denying Christ, all right. But you said 'essential point.'" He paused, then raised his voice. "*Nee*-chuh"— he pronounced it the German way—"is fundamentally exposing the contradiction between talent and mass society."

There were private smiles around the table and nervous glances at me. It suddenly dawned on me these were enemies of democracy and admirers of Hitler. And despite my uniform, I'd disappointed them with my liberalism.

Yet Bud seemed to like me no matter what I said. He sought me out afterward. "Lieutenant," he boomed. "Glad to see fascism hasn't diminished the rigor of scholarship. One hears stories, you know." Then more softly: "Your points were well-taken."

"I was afraid you would be thinking me—how does man say?—*überholt.*"

"Outdated? On the contrary!" He winked. "Call me Bud."

"And you call me Fred, please." This was the first time I'd offered this inanity, but when out West…

He shook my hand. "Got yourself a deal, Fred."

The following week he cornered me after a debate about Spencer. "Say, Fred, I've got someone I want you to meet, and she's a close relative."

"A beautiful daughter?" I teased.

"How'd ya know?" he chuckled. "Yeah, Helen's with us for the summer—studying down in Boulder—bright gal, lots of pep. Thought the two of you might hit it off."

Was everyone ignoring my status? "Well, I am not knowing what companion I make, Bud. Do you forget I am POW?"

He smiled. "Well, yeah, I suppose you are." He shot me a conspiratorial glance. "Look, why don'tcha leave the paperwork to me? You two just have a good time."

♦

[Somewhere in Lawndale the next year, 18-year-old Marilyn would discuss her career with husband Jimmy, a welder at her aircraft plant. She was massaging his back.

"So, honey, there's this Chevy dealer in the Valley that needs a girl for their 'boards."

Jimmy yawns. "How much, babe?"

"Seventy-five."

"Jesus, that's all he offered you?"

"C'mon, Jimmy…that's good money. The department stores are paying fifty…Besides, all the guys at the agencies will see it."

Jimmy writhes and her hands drop lower. "So whadda they want ya to wear, Mugs?"

"My red one."

"The *red* one? Hey, I don't know about that, babe. I'm

not so sure I want every guy on Sunset staring at your boobs every morning. Jeez, you're not even twenty-one."

Marilyn turns him over. "What's the difference, Jimmy?" she giggles. "You're the only one who…you know!"—VOB]

♦

Helen was an earlier Marilyn—young, curvaceous, with shaped blonde hair and a wispy air. Long before I could have known, she also had M's flirtatiousness. (I was the only one who wept at the debut of *Gentlemen Prefer Blondes*.) Yet politically, she was Daddy's Girl—as relentless a fascist as Bud was. But it was a homespun fascism that would steal upon you.

That first meeting in the gazebo, tended by her apple tree, when I could have sworn she'd been swimming nude—the droplets on her body winking at the sunshine, the white robe wrapped tightly, the turquoise of the pool.

She peered up the hill after reaching me. "Well, I hope you couldn't see that far." Then facing me: "I generally don't strip for strangers."

I decided to gamble. "Then why *did* you?"

No pause. "Couldn't resist the feeling." She chose an opposite bench. "Of the water, that is. Have a boyfriend at school."

Didn't believe her. Or rather what she had didn't matter. I extended my hand. "Fred Dassen."

She took it lightly. "Dassen, hmm—doesn't that mean existence or something?"

"*Nein!*" I laughed, "that's *Dasein!*"

"Oh, too bad. There's a girl on campus who goes around calling herself 'Ellie Existentialist.'"

"Clever."

"No, Jewish." "Jewish" was said with a trace of contempt, and my stomach turned slightly. Why had I imagined her an impish socialist, goading her father with quotes from Debs?

I changed the subject. "What is the cooking for dinner?" There was charcoal in the air.

"Pot roast. Mom's best dish when she was alive."

It was the first I'd heard of Grace's death. I bowed my head. "I am not knowing about your mother. Bud is not telling me this."

She drifted. "Yah, voted for Willkie, then went to sleep." She swallowed, surprised the grief was still fresh. She pointed to a ridge. "She's buried over there."

I sighed. "*Ja*, I never knew my father. First War."

"Oh, sorry." Then brightened: "Tell me about your mother, then."

♦

Bud was out of sorts that night—the headline of the local paper screamed "Reds on the March—Nazis Yield Orel." "Well, I lived to see the day," he growled, "when the *Press* prints Red propaganda."

"Now, Bud, you're not denying Orel fell?" It was his neighbor Karl, who had joined us for dinner.

"Hell, no, Karl." He picked up the paper and slapped it. "But 'Reds on the March'? What's that? I mean, what are we—the Third International cheering Stalin's march to Berlin?"

Karl cut his meat. "Well, the sooner Hitler falls, the quicker our boy will be home. That's the way Edith and I see it."

Bud's jaw tightened. "Yeah? Home to what? The Russians in half of Europe?" He returned to his paper. "I think we'd better be thinking of changing sides here right quick." He pointed to me. "Helping these people defend themselves."

Eyes turned to me. "Well, eventually," I smiled.

"Sooner rather than later, right?" Bud coaxed.

Helen defended me. "Fred's one of those Germans who doesn't like Hitler, Daddy."

Karl nodded at me. "I don't think most *do* anymore."

Bud gulped his seltzer. "Yeah well, Hitler's made mistakes—there's some rashness there. But the campaign against the Soviets—that was yeoman work."

After dinner, Helen and I exchanged anecdotes, mainly involving her sorority and my military training. She loved the story of how my pal Eric, suffering a hangover, was about to join formation without his tie. Suddenly realizing the oversight, with the inspector closing in, he removed his right sock and tied it round his neck. The sock was grey, the inspector myopic—Eric got away with it!

But I never divulged Mother's politics to the Hoffmans—not only would it have upset them, but if it got back to camp, it might have compromised me. The *Lagergestapo* executed over 250 POWs in the U.S. True, no officers but one never knew—socialists and Communists were targets, after all. Yet I spoke freely about my distaste for fascism—on that matter, I felt safer.

Yet politics wasn't the issue in this Tale of Hoffman. It was eugenics.

6

The visit came that Tuesday. I was hiking past the Schiller farm when I noticed a man peering under the hood of a Packard. I volunteered to help.

He slammed the hood closed. "That won't be necessary, Dassen. I'm here to help *you*."

"How are you knowing my name?"

He offered his hand. "Lenny Hart, Denver stringer for the *Worker*."

"*The Daily Worker?* That's a Communist paper."

He pointed to the orchards. "Red as the apples." Then smirked.

I became alarmed. "Mr. Hart, I am POW here—you cannot write me in your paper!"

He lowered his voice: "I have a letter from your mother. Smuggled by a comrade to Sweden, then mailed from New York." He handed me the envelope, I recognized the writing.

I looked around, then stuffed it in my jacket. "Thank you, Mr. Hart." I was a little ashamed about my outburst. "I am sorry for—"

"*Das Mißtrauen?*" He knew his German. He patted my shoulder. "Hey, don't worry about it, Lieutenant.

Suspicion's an occupational hazard."

A tractor appeared at the crest. I covered myself. "*Ja*, you go down this road, mister, just to the stop sign there. Then at the highway, you are turning left."

He hopped into his car. "Thanks, kid." Then winked. "You'll be home sooner than you think."

♦

I saved the letter for after dinner. What I dreaded was any reference to "climbing"—which, by code meant sabotage against the Reich.

I lay on my bunk and tipped the lampshade. Thunder roared in the distance.

6 July

Hübschmann [Handsome One],

Everything has changed—nothing is the same as it was. Now the true Hitler is known. Yes, a fascist enslaving the working class, without the refinements of democracy. Yes, an assassin of Communists and socialists. Yes, an imperialist colonizing Europe.

But now far worse: a global murderer, a twentieth-century Satan exterminating '*die Untermenschen* [Subhumans]'. This is beyond politics—this is *der Rassenmord* [genocide]!

They will tell you these reports are lies—enemy propaganda. Don't believe it—they are true. Soviet comrades have witnessed scores of 'clean-ups' in their towns and villages. Comrades in Germany, working in the hearths, confirm that ovens have been designed for 5000 bodies daily. (Do not doubt this—I have seen the blueprints.)

WHY??? Even from a fascist perspective, or an imperialist one, such murder is unnecessary. It's only required of a vampire...or a vampire state, which I suppose is what we've become.

I rack my brain guessing the root of this brutality. It cannot be Hitler alone. You're the philosopher— tell me: was it Luther, Hegel, Nietzsche, Treitschke? WHO VITIATED US?

So I've taken up climbing, risky as it is. Frankly, having witnessed fascism has dulled my taste for life. You may choose to return to this *Schlacthaus* [slaughterhouse]—I don't think I'd be a cheerful grandma. I leave that to the chameleons of my generation who, I suppose, will be good liberals later as they are good Nazis now.

I received your card from Norfolk and am pleased you're in Teton—given the casualties in Russia, you're a fortunate soldier. It's beautiful in the mountains, *nicht?* Frau Zimmer has relatives in Denver.

Remember me,
Mother

♦

I didn't sleep well that night—I had the feeling I was living in history's loony bin. In contemplating Mother's letter, I began to lose my grip. I heard high-pitched sounds and voices jabbering. I felt my bed rise. I smelled bodies burning.

Intuitively the next morning, I sought out Captain Rausch. His eyes were bloodshot—had no one slept that night?

I sat at his desk crestfallen. He addressed me gently. "Lieutenant, is something wrong?"

I spoke softly. "There are rumors, Captain."

"Rumors?"

"Atrocities."

"Ours or theirs?"

I caught his eyes. "Ours."

"Individual cases?" I shook my head. He squirmed. "What is it you want from me, Lieutenant?" I looked down. He grew impatient. "Look, man, I'm not at the front! I know no more than you do!"

I kept my head down, then heard him sigh. He shuffled over to his file cabinet—I followed him with my eyes. He removed a folder, then lifted a clipping from it. It was from the *New York Times*.

He raised his voice. "Who do you wish to believe— *Der Beobachter* or"—he peered at the clipping—"Rabbi Iz-rayel Gold-stein from Temple Buh-nay Jesh-oorun?" He struggled with the Hebrew.

I looked up. "The rabbi."

He dropped his hands on his desk. "Very well." He paused. "The rabbi believes two million Jews have been killed."

"And Poles? And Gypsies?"

"Lieutenant, please."

"IS IT TRUE, CAPTAIN?"

He sighed, then threw up his hands. *"Der Führer* is mad. *'Das Herrenvolk, die Untermenschen* [The Master Race, subhumans]' ..." His voice trailed off. The first chill of fall whistled in the alley.

♦

Corporal Schultz was a POW across the road. He'd been a postman in Stuttgart, where his parents had been Social Democrats. Prior to entering politics, his father had risen in the miner's union.

He was in his late twenties—short, slight, with an oval face—the kind of guy you might bury in an envelope. I found him cringing outside my cottage one morning, chaperoned by an American sergeant, who saluted me, as their NCOs often did. Schultz did so as well, in his cowering way.

"Lieutenant Dassen?" the Yank asked.

I tried to sound official. "Sergeant?"

He pointed to his charge. "This is Corporal Schultz, 14th Regiment, who's experiencing 'social difficulties' in Block 12. Captain Rausch asks you to assist."

I turned towards the German. "Difficulty, Corporal? What kind?"

The corporal's eyes met mine. *"Politisch, Leutnant."*

Politics, damn. The last thing I wanted was to become Father Confessor to anti-Nazis across the road. I took the sergeant aside. "May I speak with the corporal privately?"

The Yank shrugged. "Your call, Lieutenant."

I felt safe advising Schultz in my cottage—my house-mates were in the woodshop. The sergeant kept sentry.

"What's this all about, Corporal?" We were in German now—Schultz on the sofa, me in the armchair.

He looked down. "You know *die Lagergestapo?*" I nodded knowingly. But all I knew is what Rausch had told me. "They've targeted me."

"For what?"

"They claim I divulged code when Tommy grilled us in Tunis."

He worried me—he had that earnest naïveté thugs like to torment. "Well, did you?"

"Did I what?"

"Divulge code." My memory was that the Brits had cracked our script earlier in the year.

"Of course not. But they worked me over for six hours." Then he got down to tacks—as an alderman, his father had resisted the Nazis. One of the *Lager* punks was from his town.

"Have they threatened you?"

"Who?"

"The *LG.*"

He shook his head. "No. Just told me they know I sung to Tommy."

"And?"

He looked down. "Told me I'd better be careful—not get too cozy with the Yanks."

I paused. "Well, don't."

♦

During the day, I labored over my project—my search for the Axiom. My desk overlooked a brook that threaded the hillside like an errant stitch. A captain in my cottage was a physicist, and I kept him up nights with cosmic questions. But I made little progress.

Later that week the infirmary became concerned about my pulse and referred to me to Shelburne for an EKG. The next morning a guard drove me to the hospital, where I passed the exam. ("False alarm, Lieutenant—you'll live to be one-hundred.") Upon returning, I found a note from Helen on stationery from a Munich hotel:

Lieber Kamerad!

Word has it you require treatment. My diagnosis: you suffer from *ein Überherz* [a superheart]. Will you submit to examination?

Grüße,
Nurse H.

The note confirmed what I always sensed—the Hoffmans were well-connected in the county. Although they never mentioned sources, they always seemed to know what was happening. This hardly bothered me—it may have been Bud, after all, who persuaded the camp to cancel my escort. *("Leave the paperwork to me. The two of you just have fun.")*

There was a pond behind Bud's home, a haven for ducks. Beside it were a bench and two armchairs, painted baby blue. I remember Helen in the breeze that afternoon, a bed of lilacs behind her, the leaves of an elm dappling her uniform. And a stethoscope in her lap. *Ecce Medicus.*

No words were exchanged. I sat on the bench as the wind billowed. She placed the prongs in her ears, then unbuttoned my shirt, slowly, willfully. I took a breath. She reached over my shoulders and pressed the sensor to my heart.

There was chemistry and foreboding. It was *der Sturm* all over again: the rallies of '30, the blaring speakers, the hint of hegemony…and the pleading voice. She licked my shoulders, her nails on my chest. She threw off the detector, I ripped off my pants. Then she was inside my waistband and I kicked off my shorts. But her palm returned, oscillating lazily. And all the while her tongue on my back, tracing my spine.

I was suddenly savage and led her downward. I conjured cattle, mountain bovines. But she stopped me with a whisper. "Not here, darling." She dropped to her knees and swallowed me. (So this was the "blowjob" the sergeants raved about.) I dug my hands into her shoulders, arching towards her.

Was this real?—wild in the Antlers, Mother a guerrilla, fascism beneath me…mother for the sickle, Helen for the swastika, and that same demented cross pinned to my pocket? All I ever wanted was to teach logic on a quiet campus. But not to be, dear reader: no logic, no college, no silence…

♦

For weeks it seemed sex was all we did—the entire fall, a mating season. I look back at my dairy and "Ranch" is entered daily.

After lunch in the mess, I'd wander to the road and kickstart the scooter she'd given me. Then out to the highway, a ribbon of tar through the raucous autumn. She had her own cottage on the ranch and I'd circle it noisily, then brake on her doormat. There she'd be, like a pinup on the wall, with her blouse unbuttoned and the door ajar.

"Aryan Angel" she called me, and, yes, it bothered me, but you must understand: all my life others had gone to dances, met in bars, skinny-dipped in lakes, fucked in the forests. They'd written secret letters to married women and married secret women in letters. They were sleazy and sneaky, and now it was my turn—*ja*, my turn to sip Campbell's with a smirk, then slip out of camp unnoticed.

Remember, Helen? You're lying on my chest and you're talking weather. You're droning on about early blizzards and Chinooks that melt snowmen. And I'm not caring what it is, you could be talking spark plugs. All I know is I'll soon recover and bend you towards me.

But there were complications. Like contraception. Or the lack of it. Like the first time we made love and I reached for my Trojan.

"What do you need that for?" you laughed, perhaps a

bit derisively.

"To stop you from becoming the Mama."

You considered me crazy. "Why?"

I was hard-pressed to answer. What was I guarding?—the career I hadn't chosen? the fiancée I didn't have? the account with nothing in it? I leaned back on the pillow and sighed. "Sweetheart, I am just not knowing if I am ready—"

"For what, darling?"

I stared at her. "Well, to have…to be—"

"A father?" She smiled. "You won't *have* to be, angel— I'll be the Mommy, Bud'll be the Daddy!"

"You want this?"

"A child? Sure. Doesn't every girl?"

"You are not wanting some American guy, to be married in a house? I mean, after the war?"

"After the war?" There was contempt in her voice. "I've heard this for years now. This war will never end!"

I tried to sound responsible. "*Ja* but Helen, I must be careful. No matter what you say, it can be my fault."

You wrapped your arms around my neck. "Look, Freddy, I don't want no American guy, no ranch boy with dirty nails. I want my angel."

"But—"

You placed your finger over my lips. "Shhh. Daddy has a lawyer. We'll take care of this. When it's over, Freddy can go back home! No strings attached!"

"Helen, I—"

"FUCK ME, *LEUTNANT*!"

♦

Shelburne is the seat of the county that bears its name, but what makes the town unique is that, despite being WASP, it considers itself ethnic. It seems the Brits who settled the place arrived later than the colonists—more than two centuries later, if you're counting from Jamestown. So they view themselves as hyphenated Americans—Anglo-Americans, if you will.

Walk the town after dark and you're likely to find Victorian pubs dishing out Yorkshire pudding and shepherd's pie. And pumping rounds of Guinness.

Not that I was pubbing after my chat with Helen. No, I was in the office of Representative Gene Dobbs, who just happened to be Bud's attorney. The barrister sat behind a mammoth desk—it looked like an entire oak had been felled for it. Outside, red leaves brushed the window.

"How's your English, Lieutenant?" In Germany, a provincial lawyer would be short and fat, with pink cheeks from beer and snow. But here in Teton, lawyers looked like Gable—tall, lean, athletic.

"Quite fine, Counsel." I'd learned this term from the dictionary.

He smiled broadly. "Swell." He swiveled toward the window and leaned back. "Lieutenant, I can't impress upon you too strongly how confidential—" he checked with me—"you know what I mean by that?'"

"Important?"

"Well, no..." He wheeled toward me. "Secret. *Geheim.*"

"*Ach so.*"

67

"Yes, Mr. Hoffman and his daughter—well, let's start with you, Lieutenant. You're a German prisoner, an alien—" He raised his hand. "I understand the mitigating circumstances—the quality of your education, your status as an officer, your regard for our way of life…your, er, appearance and demeanor, which has drawn Miss Hoffman—"

"You speak me too good, Counsel." I was blushing.

"Well, no, we're both adults here, we need to be frank…But you must understand: should there be any, er, consequence to this liaison, it's vital your identity never be revealed—indeed that your paternity enjoy no confirmation." I nodded. "Now, Miss Hoffman tells me you're agreeable to such terms."

"*Ja*, but—"

"But what, Lieutenant?"

"Can this be done, er, before the hand?"

Dobbs chuckled. "Well, I hope I've gone to law school!" He ruffled through some papers and removed two sheets. "Actually, surrender of paternity has become quite common in these parts—what with the Depression and now the War. *Pre facto*, I'll grant you, is irregular but, of course, the principles of law remain the same." He handed me the documents. "There's one in English, one in German, just so there's no misunderstanding." He pointed down the hall. "Now I'm going to walk you over to my partner's office, and I want you to look these over—take as long as you like. When you're finished, just let my girl know and we'll have you back in to sign…"

7

I never returned to Bates' group after the talk on Spencer—the not-so-hidden agenda made me uneasy. The only time I spent with Bud was at Sunday dinners at Helen's.

Bud reveled in anticipating his grandchild. Helen fed these expectations by coy references to the "Little One," "the Baby Jesus," or the "Aryan Warrior." Bud would mourn the retreat from Kiev and Helen would stretch, yawn, then tease her father: "Soon comes the Warrior, Papa!" He would raise a glass, search her eyes, then faintly smile.

As you might imagine, I felt superfluous at these moments. What was I, after all—some German stud sent to impregnate the fascist queen? (I, who learned *das Zärtlichkeit* [tenderness] at Helga's knee!)

This mythology of theirs escalated at Christmas, and so did my discomfort. As usual, Helen led the toast. "To the Sapient Child."

His glass kissed hers. "Awaited. Expected."

The glasses clinked. "To lead us from the Morass..."

"To forge the New Order…"

"What goes wrong with the one you have?" I asked sharply. This was the first time I'd crossed swords with

Bud. Previously, I'd been content to establish distance.

Bud was unfazed. He imbibed his wine, then gently placed his glass on the table. Then looked me in the eyes. "It can be improved upon, Fred."

Helen lowered her glass. She wasn't going to smooth things over. The rams must sort it out.

I kept coming. "Oh, so great. You and your friends will decide who lives and who dies. Line 'em up and shoot 'em, right?" My voice cracked. "OR SHOULD WE HAVE OVENS IN TETON LIKE THEY ARE HAVING IN POLAND?"

I threw down my napkin and headed for the door. I grabbed my coat, then rushed into the snow. There were tears in my eyes.

He followed me into the whiteness—I heard him running behind me. "Fred!…man, please!"

He caught up to me. "Leave me alone!" I cried.

"C'mon, it's cold out here! Let's go over to my office and talk this thing over."

"I don't want to talk!"

"C'mon, Fred. Helen will never forgive me. Have a heart."

I stopped in my tracks. Where the hell was I going—into a snowbank? I sighed, then conceded. "Okay, Bud. Okay."

His office was in a separate cabin—"A man shouldn't work where he sleeps," he used to say. We shook the snow off our boots. There was a faded rug on the floor. He lit a fire and we drew our armchairs around it.

He was an expert woodsman—the flames were ferocious. We retreated from the hearth. All day I'd been thinking of Mother—was she torching factories? Had they caught her?

The wood cackled in the silence. "Look, the way I see it, Fred, we couldn't have become human without fire." He poked a log. "We could trek into the Cold Beyond. But without fire, we'd've gone as apes." He shook his head. "No, you can't have community without the fireside—not in the North anyway."

I cut the poem short—I had no time for anthropology. I looked him in the eyes. "Bud, Hitler is exterminating people."

I expected him to discount it, as apologists were doing. But he surprised me. "I've heard that," he said softly.

"You think it's okay?"

He looked down. "If it's true, it's wrong."

"Just wrong?"

He raised his head. "If it can be proved, it's a crime. Against the rules of war."

"I was thinking you would favor it."

He shot me a wounded glance. "Well, I believe in Aryan leadership, but—"

"But what?"

He stood up to push a log, then returned to his chair. I searched him for a reply. "Look, I don't believe in killing civilians, okay?" he said impatiently.

I relaxed. Why was I fighting these folks? Helen wanted to snuggle under the covers, bear my child. Bud was nuts, but when you came right down to it, what was he?—just another cowboy scared of the Reds.

But then the pitch came.

I remember the glass of brandy in my hand, which Bud kept refreshing, and the flame. And the brown lithographs of pioneers on the wall, with their covered wagons and Levis.

"Look, Fred, it's like this." There was an air of finality to his voice, as if everything since July had been child's play. He cleared his throat. "Six thousand years ago, near the mouth of the Volga, the original Aryan chiefs communed with their destiny."

"Destiny?"

"Yeah, they got their assignment—I don't know how else to put it. I'm not trying to be dramatic. It's just that after remaining localized for centuries, they just, well, marched on the world—east to found Persia and India, West to remake Europe."

I suddenly understood him. "Ah, *ihre Aufgabe*. They are learning their task."

"*Ja, ihre Aufgabe*." His accent wasn't bad. "Now they didn't have blond hair and blue eyes like Hitler implies—they probably looked like, I don't know, Ukranians might today. They didn't speak a Semitic language—they spoke the original Indo-European tongue, which they probably learned from hunters in the Urals. For example, their word for fondness was *prei*—the root of the English words 'friend' and 'free.'"

"*Ach so*," I confirmed. "And the German words *Freund* and *Frei*."

Bud sipped his brandy. "Right…Now what they also learned from the mountain folk was how to breed and ride faster horses. I say faster because, well, they had nothing like the race horses we have today, which can gallop, what, thirty miles per hour. But, well, theirs could probably trot ten to 15.

"And that gave them a tremendous military advantage. Because when they hitched these steeds to spoked carts, they essentially devised the first cavalry. And it was that cavalry which over the next three millennia overwhelmed most of the indigenous people of Europe…and many of the peoples of central Asia."

He leaned forward. "Now, these indigenous peoples, Fred—well, in Europe they'd be the ancestors of, say, the Basques—you can call them the 'Old Europeans' if you like: they were skilled potters and weavers, but in the end no match for Aryan horsemen and their weapons."

"Weapons?" I asked.

"Yeah, the Aryans wielded axes, swords, shields, spears, javelins, daggers. Their cavalry, like I said, at first employed carts…but those eventually became forbidding chariots. The Old Europeans had none of these things."

"An uneven match."

He chuckled. "Yeah, very uneven…Well, of course, the rest is history. By the third millennium, the Aryans were in Sweden, by 2500 B.C. in Ireland, by 1500 B.C. in northern India." He looked me in the eyes. "But it's in Greece, of course, that their genius is revealed." He walked over to the wall and pulled down a world map.

"Consider human civilization at the time of Pythagoras and Heraclitus, five centuries before Christ." He pointed to Mesopotamia. "The Babylonians boast the most advanced civilization in the world, but their theology and mathematics are static. Inspired by the prophet Isaiah, the Jews have already envisioned a global spiritual community ruled by a Prince of Peace…but they show little talent for science, theater, art.

"On to this stage saunters Greek intellect, and the world has never been the same. Compared to the empires of Babylon, Egypt, or China, the Greeks were a hodgepodge of small ports, without fancy palaces and huge armies. But from these modest towns, they fashion the leading philosophy, science, and theater of the ancient world.

"Take mathematics. Pythagoras founds the scientific dialectic of bold theory and logical demonstration. By the third century B.C., Euclid publishes his geometrical axioms.

"Now, the Babylonians had been deploying quadratic equations, exponents, cube roots—even some geometric formulas—but they saw no need for a systematic approach to geometry—no need, in fact, for systematic methodology of any kind." He stared at me, I blinked. "What was going on here? Why were these intrepid Greeks from these craggy inlets overtaking Babylon's scribes?"

He retook his seat and refilled our glasses. The coals of the fire reddened. "Look, Fred, I don't buy that Nazi crap—I don't believe Aryans possess superior intelligence. Whatever genetic differences there are between peoples is probably not terribly significant. But I *do* believe the way Aryans have developed socially enables us to perform better than other cultures…and until others array in similar fashion, humanity is best off following our lead."

I sipped my brandy while he continued. "Now, of course, besides mathematics, there were breakthroughs on other fronts in Greece. In biology and botany—the research of Aristotle. In social theory—Plato's plea for intellectual aristocracy. And theater—oh, theater!—where Aeschylus, Sophocles, and Euripedes pioneer a bold new art form: a sort of psychoanalysis, where subconscious contradictions are located, then resolved."

His remarks on theater surprised me—I hadn't thought him capable of such insight. But I'd seen *Medea* in Berlin and agreed with him.

He revived the flames with a couple of logs and returned to his chair. Helen had likely given up on us and curled up with a book. "Now, you might ask: why Greece? Why the Aryans? Well, I have a number of theories. First of all, the Mediterranean climate is invigorating. You can see here it here on the plateau: autumn comes and the ranchers come alive with all sorts of schemes. Well, they have a long autumn and spring in Greece.

"And of course, the fact that Greece was a mercantile nation put it in touch with the ancient wisdom and knowledge of Egypt and Phoenicia…and perhaps through these intercessors, Mesopotamia as well.

"But what I think was crucial was the relationship between government, theology, and intellect in Greece. In the Semitic theocracies—Babylon, Egypt, Judea—intellectuals were cowed by the domineering worldview of palace or priesthood: they would trim their outlook to the narrow concepts of superiors.

"But in ancient Aryan societies, intellectuals were aristocrats descended from the warrior cavalry. And the Aryan tradition had been that the warrior on horseback was not answerable to the priesthood—intellectually or economically. His right to his own theology, cosmology, or politics was lineal.

"This proved a vital difference in comparison to Semitic culture. In most cases it enabled Greek cities to resist theocracy and monarchy. And it encouraged intellectuals (first in Ionia, and then in the rest of Greece) to pioneer a new science and psychology.

"Granted, the politics was often oligarchic and the religion increasingly a comedy of anthropomorphic gods, who were more amusing than authoritative. But the science was increasingly methodological, requiring bold theory followed by logical proof. And the collective psychology—Oedipus bedding his mother, Medea strangling her sons: nothing less than courageous confrontation of demons of the soul.

"Then Greece goes global—takes it all on the road. In the late fourth century B.C., Aristotle's pupil, the Macedonian prince Alexander, accedes to the throne...then carries Hellenic culture as far south as Egypt, as far east as the Punjab. After his death, one of his generals, Seleucus Nicator, establishes a dynasty in Syria that undertakes a century later to Hellenize Palestine.

"That undertaking inevitably pits Hellenism against Judaism—one of history's most poignant contests. On one hand, the Seleucid overlords in Antioch: exercising nude in their gymnasia…attending analytic drama in their amphitheaters…disputing philosophy, mathematics, and science in their academies; on the other, the pale seminarians in Jerusalem keenly conscious of their national history and epic dialogue with an abstract God.

"It's at this historical instant that the West confronts its fork in the road: which of these two powerful agenda will guide its future? The Aryan?—physical, secular, rational, theoretical, scientific, analytic, dramatic, anarchic; or the Jewish?—sedentary, repressed, theocratic, mystical, canonic, pious.

"Sounds like an easy choice, doesn't it? And in fact, upper-class Jewish youth at first flocked to the Syrian centers of Damascus and Aleppo. But then came the Maccabean backlash in Judea, where patriots and fundamentalists teamed up against the cosmopolitan upper class and Greek occupation. It is in this context that Joshua of Nazareth would later fashion a third alternative—neither patriotic nor dogmatic nor cosmopolitan…but rather a new kind of spirituality, partly influenced by the Orient."

The brandy had dipped below the label. The fire was a chorus of embers, which Bud no longer conducted. The sun sank behind the hill. My teacher leaned towards me. "Yet the point, Fred, isn't how Jesus differed with Jewish theocrats—the point is he *was* a theocrat, once again placing revelation above carnality, theater, reason, science, theory. In the final analysis, Jesus was a Semite. Of course, he was—what else could he be?"

"But the Romans are going for it!" I protested. "They are becoming Christian!"

He lifted his palms defensively. "Yes, they did! But the question is *why*. How could western Aryan civilization, which at first so impressed Jewish intellectuals—which literally *commanded* Jewish culture for a time—how could it lose its nerve in the fourth century and surrender Reason?"

"Because they go Christian?" He nodded. "Was that so bad?"

"Well, it was understandable. Part of the Roman elite seems to have lost its mind in the first century—too much power, too much wealth. Caligula is symptomatic—capricious, tyrannical, exploitative. Marrying his goddam horse!" He laughed out loud, then shook his head. "Such a tragedy. The Roman elite had been so successful in the material world—in engineering, administration. But they seemed incapable of acknowledging limits—the *boundaries* of power.

"They tried to reconcile themselves to reality in the second century with their philosopher-emperor, Aurelius, but ultimately Stoicism wasn't something soldiers would die for. And when you're facing chronic invasion, what soldiers will die for is important."

"Roman soldiers are not dying for Jesus either," I noted.

"Well, they did in Constantinople, which, as you know, resisted the Turks until the fifteenth century. The point is, for whatever reason—a decadent aristocracy, a resentful laboring class—western Aryan civilization struck a Faustian bargain with Semitic civilization. And that bargain was revelatory theology.

"In the sixteenth and seventeenth centuries, western Aryan culture would partly recover, thanks partly to the fact the Hindus and Muslims had tended mathematics. It revived its science with Galileo, Newton, Leibniz, Descartes. And its theater with Shakespeare and Racine. And by the eighteenth century, it would add the profound music of Bach, Mozart, Beethoven."

He patted my shoulder. "We're almost home, son. All we've got left is Nietzsche and Marx."

He stood up—the final salvo would be a lecture. "You see, with Nietzsche and Marx, we once again confront the dispute between Hellenism and Judaism. Never mind the fact the young Marx was rhetorically antisemitic, attacking the Jews for separating themselves from mankind. The fact is he went on to oppose Aryan enterprise on moral grounds…in the same way Christians had disparaged Roman power.

"As you well know, Nietzsche opposed revelatory socialism…contrived egalitarianism. Like the aristocrat Heraclitis, he warned socialists that life in this cosmos was competitive, ennobled only by the extraordinary wisdom or artistry of individual genius."

"Der Übermensch ..."

"Well, the concept of Overman, yes. The notion that the human venture is not just a game of bingo—counting dollars, counting noses. It's about breakthrough—exceptional, elegant breakthrough."

Bud slumped in his chair as if he'd finished a marathon. Then hissed like a punctured tire. He turned towards me wearily. "Fred, do you see what I'm driving at?"

It'd been such a *tour de force*, I could hardly speak.

♦

Back in '35, three physicists—Einstein, Podolsky, and Rosen—deduced a curious property of quantum reality. Two particles from the same source—even though galaxies apart—might be "correlated" pairs: if one registered a given positive position and momentum, its twin would boast the matching negative position and momentum.

In retrospect, this is how I see Marilyn Monroe and Helen Hoffman.

Marilyn was the left-wing blonde...or *would* be by the time her position and momentum were significant enough to measure. The Marxian particle. She would study under Strasberg, marry Miller, then tease Camelot just before suicide.

Helen would prove as reckless. But she was the right-wing blonde—the fascist particle spinning towards Aryan hegemony.

And I, the survivor, who chose neither swastika nor sickle, who delighted in lying beneath the aspens—the cavernous kiss, her nipple in my teeth, the clenched hand lifting the buttock...

Ah, but what is their common source, their elusive parent? It is that Queen of Sparta, whom the Trojan Prince abducted, then lost to the Amphictyony.

♦

There came a time I had to know.

"Is it because of Bud?" I asked, stretching lazily under her covers.

"You mean, my politics?" she asked, talking to the ceiling. I nodded. She shook her head. "I'm my own girl, Fred. You know that."

"But Bud is so—"

"I admire my father: his erudition, his diligence, the way he"—she sliced the air with her hand—"cuts to the quick." She faced me. "You know? No nonsense, no patience for fools."

I propped myself with a pillow. "But what do you want to do, Helen—kill Jews?"

She sighed. "No, I..." Her voice trailed off.

"You don't have to say me."

"No, it's no secret, Fred." She propped herself as well. "How can I explain?...Look, I was in high school with a German girl named Eva and a Polish girl named Olga. We were studying together in an empty classroom...after school, I guess...geometry. And the concept of π—the ratio of a circle's circumference to its diameter—what's it, 3.14? Well, Olga, who certainly was as bright as were—in history, literature, even biology—she just couldn't grasp the concept that a curved shape could be approximated in linear terms. I mean, no matter how we tried to explain it, she wasn't able—

"It was for her maybe a bad day."

"Oh, there could be lots of reasons, Freddie. I mean, maybe she had a block about circles." Then folded her arms. "But that's not how it felt." There was a silence; I almost couldn't go on. "It was then I realized that Dad was right—at least, conceivably. There *could* be neurological patterns that are genetically acquired."

"By who?"

"Well, by Aryans, silly!"

♦

The inevitable herald:

The door to her cottage is open and I tiptoe to her couch, wondering if she's still napping. We're all getting drowsy in the Alpine spring as an insurgent sun overthrows the winter. "APRIL FOOL!" she shouts, and I notice a bulbous nose in the mirror. It's Helen in her clown costume.

"April Scherz!" I greet her.

"April *what*, sweetie?

I face the harlequin. "In Germany, we're not saying 'April Fool.' We're saying 'April Joke.'"

She takes off her nose and sits on the couch, waving me into the Morris chair. "Oh, I get it. You put the emphasis on Prank rather than Prankster."

"Something like that. In France, they say *'Avril Poisson.'"*

She puts the nose on the coffee table. "April *Person?*" She knows no French.

"No, April *Fish!* See, this is all beginning when they are changing calendar in the Renaissance. The Pope is erasing two weeks to match the calendar with the sky. But some of the boys that carry the fish cannot follow. So the grocers are making fun of them."

"How are they making fun of them?"

"By telling them to carry the fish by, er, 7 April when already it's, er, 21 April!"

She scratches her head. "Wait a second. Are these delivery boys?"

"*Ja*, errand boys for the grocers."

"Ah, and they can't figure out the new calendar, right? I mean, that's what's going on here?" I nod. She points at me. "Got it. April Fish."

And then the Teton silence, pierced by the chirp of a magpie.

"I'm pregnant, Friedrich."

"Oh, *mein Gott!*" I blurt. "Oh, *mein Gott!*" Then deep breath. "HELEN...*WUNDERBAR!*" (Should I have proposed? Yet it wasn't love nor was meant to be.)

"Daddy's ecstatic."

"*Ja*, of course! And so I am, so will be everyone!" There were tears in my eyes. I beckoned her towards me. "Come here, *mein Hanswurst* [traditional German clown]! Give your *Leutnant* a kiss..."

8

Afterwards, everything quickened. It was as if the world had been slogging through a gaunt pond, then suddenly hit the rapids. There had to be resolution, there couldn't be hesitation.

And so the onslaught. On the Eastern front, the frenzied Reds loosing the grip on Warsaw and Budapest. (After that, only elegant Prague separating them from Berlin.) To the West, Normandy…and Paris.

Meanwhile, my Tale of Hoffman lurched towards tragedy. I couldn't stop it—I found no escape from the global madhouse. Nazis, Reds—their contest overwhelmed me. There was no common ground on which a peacemaker might build his study. Yet study I did.

No, I didn't control events, I contended with them. I was scholar, lover, and again briefly soldier as I balanced liberalism with angst.

And you who'd have done it differently: look, there's no Hitler, Stalin, or Tojo in this world and a liberal sits in the White House. This is my gift, I belong to that dole, I'm part of the system that made that outcome. Change me, bar me from the Wehrmacht, throw me from her bed, evade the Warrior—change any of the variables and you risk the *denouement.*

Gambler! How can you know how vital Helen was to fascism that year? Or how much of the German *Geist* Mother and I held hostage? Think Bach, Leibniz, Goethe, Beethoven, Rilke. We *delivered* for you, goddammit, stop second-guessing. Casualties? Terrible!—we moved when we could. It was despair that welled in '29 and it spread like a truant germ: Wall Street, Munich, Moscow—each accommodated to fallen vision. And the jets went "hsss" in Buchenwald...

Mother was a Red widow with six years internment behind her. I was a jailed scholar with a broken Underwood. We had a billion teammates, yes. And somehow the job got done.

♦

The next morning Rausch summoned me to his office. He had aged since the summer and his desk was cluttered.

"Lieutenant, there's something you should know regarding our site."

"Yes, Captain?"

"There's talk in Washington about holding classes this fall." He read from the memo. "*Ja*, 'compulsory re-education to counteract Nazi conditioning.'" He looked up at me and smiled. "A kind of indoctrination in democracy, as strange as that sounds."

"But, Captain, how will they do it? Geneva forbids it."

He shrugged. "The Americans and the British are winning the war, Lieutenant. They can do what they like."

It was at that moment I realized we were post-war—Germany was rehearsing its role as reformed partner.

"Captain, I am unable to see how—"

"It will be offered as some sort of recreational program," he interrupted. Then smirked. "'Having Fun with Democracy,'" he chuckled. "'Democracy and Baseball'…Oh well, something like that."

"Will officers participate?"

He sighed. "Lieutenant, should the program be established, I plan to propose you as an instructor. You know, political philosophy—John Locke, John Stuart Mill. The ones they like."

What could I say—that I'd fallen in with fascists? "That would certainly be a privilege, Captain. Please keep me informed."

"*Ja*, I hope it will happen." Then rubbed his forehead wearily. "Something to relieve the boredom…" He'd been a promising architect in Hamburg; a photo of his family hung on the wall.

I swallowed. "*Ja*, it must be hard, Captain."

He shuffled papers on his desk. "I get by, Lieutenant. And what of you? No woman in your life?"

"Well, Captain, as a matter of fact…"

He smiled. "Really? An American girl?" He stapled some papers. I nodded. He looked up. "Good, Dassen, good. Companionship is important."

♦

The further I plunged towards the Axiom, the more I felt the world at my sleeve—it was as if humanity feared the truth. Christianity, Judaism, fascism, Communism—did they all stand to lose?

Helen was relentless. "Daddy needs to have a talk with you, sweetheart. You really must see him."

"I'd rather be here with you."

"No, hon', this is important. You really need to stop by."

Later in her bathroom, I noticed my swastika in the mirror—recently it'd been leaping at me like a jack-in-the-box. Was I a Nazi? I'd been forced into Hitler Youth to protect my kin, coerced into War College to avoid enlistment. But who was commanding me now?

♦

Grace must have chosen Bud's sofa—it was endlessly long and white with pale blue cushions. Bud's meal had been delicious—a Holstein *schnitzel*, topped with egg and anchovy. And the wine—Wehlener Spätlese, bought before the War.

Yet my host looked ashen. "Fred, I wish to God I didn't have to break this news to you." He leaned forward in his armchair.

I replaced my glass abruptly. "What news? Is Helen all right?" I was thinking miscarriage.

He waved at me. "No, no, she's fine." He gazed at the Antlers in the twilight. "Fred, this is about Germany."

Had something happened to Mother? He couldn't possibly know. And if Berlin had surrendered…well, okay. "What about Germany?"

He clasped his hands. "Your nation's in terrible danger."

"Well, the Nazis, maybe…"

"No, no, Fred, this isn't about the Nazis. This is about the German people."

"*Ja*, the Russians may take the East and the Allies—"

"Well, that's just it, Fred. I'm not so sure there's going to be anything to take."

I bravely retook my glass. Were we heading for another marathon?

He took a deep breath. "Fred, many of America's top physicists—well, they were once in Europe—but now they're in the States. They're Jewish and—"

"So what?"

He raised his hand. "No, no, Fred, hear me out." I nodded. "There's Einstein and Bethe from Germany; Teller, Szilard, and Wigner from Hungary. Oppenheimer and Feynman are American Jews. Ulam's from Poland; Segrè and Fermi are from Italy—okay, Fermi's not Jewish, but his wife is." I shrugged my shoulders. He lowered his voice. "Fred, the Russians are barreling through Poland, but once they hit the frontier, you and I know that every *Hitlerjunge* east of Essen is gonna be lyin' down in front of those tanks. The German people will fight to the last drop. C'mon, you kiddin' me? *Communism* in Germany?"

89

I was unimpressed. "You can't stop the Red Army with kids."

He refilled his glass. "Well, that's not the way they're thinking in the Pentagon. I've talked to military men in Washington and they're expecting bitter resistance."

"Okay, resistance. So what?"

He laid his cards on the table. "The Jews talked their buddy Roosevelt into wiping Germany off the map and giving Europe to Stalin."

I nearly spat my wine. "*Nein*, America doesn't want this, Bud. Germany should be opposing Stalin after the war. America and England want the power of balance."

He ruffled through his briefcase and removed a diagram. "See this?" he pointed. "This is a blueprint for a chain-reaction bomb. Do you know anything about this stuff?"

The truth was I'd attended a weapons seminar at *die Abwehrschule*. The conclusion had been that atomic bombs were *'offener Himmel* [experimental]'—it'd take Germany a decade or more to develop them. "*Ja*, Bud, these bombs are far off for the future."

He became agitated. "Well, maybe before the Yids got to work! Hey, look, uranium bombs are here, son, and they're gonna be dropped on Germany before next summer." I turned away. "No, no, mark my words, man," he repeated. "Germany will be a rubbish heap, a goddam crater!"

His paranoia could be comical. But he was the grampa of my child and I had to humor him. "What makes you sure about this?" I asked.

He looked me in the eyes. "Fred, New York may be Jew City, but the Deep West is Patriot country. We've got people in the railroads, people in the military, we're not asleep. And neither is the Reich."

The *Reich* no less! There were certainly German agents in the U.S. But I was curious about his "Patriots." "Who is 'we'?" I asked.

He checked the door. Then softly: "The Western Patriots." He never mentioned them again.

"Bud, I, er, don't know what to say."

He got out of his chair, moved on to the hassock, then put his hand on my knee. "Fred, if I could prove to you uranium bombs are being manufactured out here in the West, would you help Helen and me stop it?"

"By *force?*"

"Well, that might be *my* choice. You'll have to ask Helen about hers."

"But I'm prisoner in this country, Bud. You know this. I'm not supposed to be off camp even!"

He raised both hands. "I know, I know. And so what we'd need from you would be symbolic."

"What means 'symbolic'?"

"*Ja, der symbolischer Beistand* [symbolic help]." I nodded. "So you'll help us?"

"*Nein!*" He turned away in disgust. "No, please, Bud, I'm not even believing America is making such bombs."

He stood up abruptly and walked over to the fire. "Fine. That's okay. No, really, I was skeptical too." Then leaned against the mantle. "So let me introduce you to a few experts, some folks who know their stuff, and you can make up your own mind." I looked away. "Come on," he insisted, "at least learn the facts...Hey," he goaded, "scholar?...evidence?"

I heaved a sighed. "All right." He grinned. I raised my index finger. "But engineers only!" I warned him. "No German agents! No U.S. Nazis!"

He snapped his fingers, then pointed at me. "Deal, Lieutenant."

♦

I was becoming enamored of my body—the "Nazi Narcissus" a mate quipped when he caught me in front of the mirror. Teton had introduced me to physical culture. First of all, the ranchers were physical with their riding, rodeos, and football. Then there were the barbells in the gym, which I was attacking regularly. And the bicycling and the hiking—it was all contributing.

For a while, I was afraid I was mimicking the auto-eroticism of the *HJ*, which loved to laud its 'blond and bronzed guys:'

Blood and bronzed guys
Aren't meant for drawing rooms.
They have to fight
And be wildly daring.
They gotta be engaged in life;
And proud, whether tall or short...

I mention this because when Helen and I performed Tantric sex I insisted on placing a mirror behind her. I wanted to observe my own body as well as hers.

It wasn't difficult persuading her to participate. "Tantra is a Hindu ritual, isn't it?" she'd asked.

"*Ja*, Bengal. You know where that is?"

"The Bengal tiger?"

"*Ja*, the Bengal tiger but that don't say me where Bengal is!" She giggled. I pointed to Calcutta on her globe. "They were doing the Tantra there at the time of Socrates."

She jumped on her couch and grabbed her legs. "I've always admired the Hindus. Sanskrit is an Aryan language."

"Absolutely. They were using the zero in the seventh century."

"Really? I thought it was the Arabs who invented the zero."

"No, the Arabs are learning it in India."

She studied the swirls in the ceiling. "Arabs in India? Oh, I suppose so. It was a Muslim who built the Taj Majal, wasn't it?" I nodded. Then: "When will we do it?"

"Next week some time." The spring sun peaked through the window and rustled the yellow in her dress. I sat on the couch and put her head on my lap. "I'm going to strip you naked," I pledged, "sit you down, and sleep inside your *yoni!*"

She put her hand on my shoulders. "You'll come too soon, sweetie!" she teased me. "You're no yogi in my *yoni!*"

We were both breathing deeply. "Watch me," I whispered.

◆

I discovered my Axiom on Midsummer's Night. I was under the stars on the camp lawn, perched on a lawn chair. I hadn't talked to anyone over dinner. One of my mates had snapped his fingers in front of my eyes: "Dassen's on his own planet again," he'd joked.

But to hell with him, I'd made my breakthrough. But I hid my notebook and told no one.

◆

"Bud, good to see ya. Lieutenant, my pleasure." Sam Williams was a lanky engineer with a shiny pair of Tony Lamas covering his shins. There was a view of Satan's Cliff from his farmhouse.

He pointed towards the couch. "Y'all have a seat." He raised a bottle of Scotch. "Hope y'all'll join me in a shot of firewater." We nodded as he poured the whisky, then extended our glasses. "Now, then, Lieutenant, how can I help ya?"

"Well, Sam," Bud interjected, "the Lieutenant here's got his doubts about the Bomb."

"Nothing *to* doubt," was the quick rejoinder. "The Bomb's here, Lieutenant. Your own people know that: Hahn, Heisenberg, von Weizsäcker…"

"Yes, I know Hahn's paper—it appeared while I was yet in Germany. Uranium, fission, of course. Heavy water may be the moderator. But there is no success in making the reaction."

Williams looked me in the eyes. "Chicago, '42. On a squash court."

My heart sank. What a specter—Hitler, Stalin, Tojo, the Americans with A-bombs—I was ready to move to Mars! But who was this guy anyway? What did he know? "How are you knowing this, Mr. Williams?"

Bud raised his hand. "Lieutenant, Sam's been gracious enough to share—"

"Can't tell you that, Lieutenant," Williams snapped. "And would deny what I've told you if anyone asked. But five years from now, you'll drive down this road and shake my hand."

I emptied my glass—I could've downed four. The engineer seemed credible to me and the following summer I knew why. It took nerve to plod on. "Mr. Williams, do you know if they are making—I mean, the Americans, are they…"

He leaned forward. "Lieutenant, if they set off a goddam chain reaction, don't you think—?"

"We'll be paying Al King a visit next week," Bud interjected.

Williams poured another shot. "Yeah, King can tell 'im what's goin' on in the Southwest. And Brown has stories about Hanford."

"Is he back yet?"

Our host sipped his spirit. "Don't know. Haven't heard a thing."

There was a long silence—for me, the Nuclear Age

had begun. "Lieutenant," drawled the engineer with sudden emotion, "I just wanna say Germany's a great nation and a bulwark against Bolshevism, which, if victorious, would spell the end of civilization. And I just pray to God—" His eyes filled with tears and his voice cracked.

"To the German people!" Bud toasted, rescuing the moment. The engineer's glass trembled as it met ours.

♦

The rusty phonograph whined scratchy sitar music. Pungent incense wafted from stained test tubes. A kerosene lamp with a violet globe hissed in the corner. In the parched heat, six roses drooped from a vase. Two gym mats served as cushions. On a silver platter between us were morsels of beef, trout, rice, and a dish of seeds, shadowed by a carafe of wine. It wasn't an ashram, but the best a POW could do.

Helen sat before me in her fourth month. Her breasts seemed fuller than usual, as if to augur motherhood. The contours of an embryo could be traced on her belly.

In the mirror behind her, I saw my own vessel—the clipped blond hair, the curved biceps, the taut abdomen. I held my breath for the requisite counts. Then shouted the required "*Phat!*" while tapping the carafe. I inhaled the wine, then droned the mantra "*devata bhava siddhaye*" while pouring glasses for Helen and myself. We each consumed portions of food, followed by sips of wine.

The phonograph dropped another record and I turned up the volume. *Tabla* began to drum, Helen's breathing quickened. With my hand on my heart, I intoned the mantra "*Shiva hum, So' hum*" ("I am Shiva. I am She."). I was boasting androgyny, as tradition demands.

I rose, walked behind her, and crouched. I moved two fingers over her heart, head, forehead, throat, ears, breasts, thighs, knees, feet, then *yoni*, chanting "*Hling, kling, kandrpa, svaha.*" My *lingam* was rigid.

Helen lay on her back, bringing her knees to her chest. I mounted and partially entered her. A half hour passed, as the record endlessly scratched.

Towards the end of our coitus, I felt a deluge of energy flow through my *lingam*. I saw a reactor in the desert split into shards. *(But* which *desert, comrade? Sonora? Chihuahua?)* I saw Helen pushing dynamite.

Yet what the August night told me was that I was destined to join them; Bud, Helen, Fred—the inseparable trio…

♦

We rode horses that summer, Captain Raubel and I, brown mustangs that Bob Brislawn was breeding near Crossroads. A couple of his mares were stabled down the road, and the wranglers let us have them on weekends.

I still remember the riverbed we used to trot through and the Indian village we found at the state line. We befriended a medicine man during our second visit, who gave Raubel an herb for his aching shoulder.

I asked the chemist how the war was affecting the village. I wasn't answered directly. "The White Man gets larger and larger," he replied, widening his eyes and extending his hands. He was a short and gaunt, this wizard, dressed in blue jeans and a T-shirt. He could have been sixty, he could have been eighty.

Raubel looked at me quizzically.

"D'ya fellas follow me?" the chemist wondered.

I asked for clarity. "Do you mean more *powerful*, Mr. er—?"

"Medicine Fox," he corrected me. "And to answer the question, I mean more arrogant."

Raubel was a little annoyed. "In what way 'arrogant'?"

The wizard gestured towards the valley. "First the guns that ran the buffalo off." He motioned towards the lake. "Then the ships that speared the whales." He pointed towards the sky. "Then the airplanes that deafened the eagle. And now…"

"Yes?" I coaxed.

"Now the bombs…" (*Gott im Himmel*, does everyone know?)

But the metaphor eluded Raubel. "Do you mean the Americans or the Germans, Mr. Fox?"

"Don't make no difference who I mean." He sealed his vial. "The demons are running wild is all."

♦

The vial helped Raubel, and we returned next weekend for more. But the wizard refused us. "If you are still hurting," he told Raubel, "you need medicine, not pharmacy."

"It is costing much?"

Fox leaned over the counter. "I don't heal for money, Captain. But the tribe is raising a schoolhouse next week. Perhaps you and the lieutenant—"

"Of course we are helping!" I interjected. Then bowed: "This is for us a privilege." The wizard nodded but Raubel was stunned: there was nothing in the Geneva Convention about building schools.

Fox's clinic sat atop a hill behind his shop. It was a small pine cabin, freshly cut—stark wood masked inside by tapestry. The weavings depicted wolves, eagles, and the tribe's namesake, the jaybird.

Raubel sat nude on a blanket of triangles. There was a pungent odor.

"It is wood chips you are burning?" I asked Fox, forgetting the word for incense.

He nodded. "Cedar, Lieutenant. Good for the muscles."

"I am not knowing the smell," I replied, but Fox was already raising his hand for silence. Then gliding his hands over Raubel's body as he intoned the mantra: "The feet…your foundation; the knees…your understanding; the thighs…your humility; the stomach…your emotions; the lungs…your freedom; the heart…your love, and the back…"—he kneaded the ailing shoulder—"your burden."

"My *burden?*" Raubel wondered.

"Yes," Fox replied, "the load you carry." Then gently: "When a soldier comes for medicine, he is nearly healed: he has taken the time, trusted advice ..." It was hypnotic, this wizardry. "But healing must be done inside you. Jay medicine is in the head. You've got to believe, Captain."

Raubel tried to look up, but Fox lowered his head. "Never look me in the eye," he cautioned. "It is through my eyes I receive the vision."

"From who?"

Fox pointed above. "The Healing Eagle." He reached for a rawhide rattle with a deerskin handle. Then to its beat repeated the slow aquiline chant:

Le'miyuh kutakya waki'yuh,
Le'miyuh shi'tay ewachu,
Le'miyuh ah'peechyuh,
Le'miyuh lo'wanyaka'yo.

[I am swooping down.
I am taking the harmful home.
I am striving to cure you.
Here I am—behold me.]

Then there was silence.

Raubel pointed to the hearth. "They are plants in the kettle?"

Fox nodded. "What we call *nuistutz*—little berry leaves that grow as vines on the mountain. We steep them in butter." Then smiled. "And you know, there's protocol for picking them. You talk to them, tell them about the person you're picking them for, lay tobacco before them, then praise them—talk about how you hope their relatives will grow strong and how people will always be

100

happy every time they see them."

"You picked the leaves for me?"

"Oh, yes." Fox looked away. "You know, in the olden days, medicine people would sit under a tree and watch their camp. Whoever went to a medicine man was told, 'I've been waiting for you.' Of course he had been—he knew how everyone was living!"

"You waited for *me*?"

"I could tell when we first met you were worn. Your ears were tired." Then resumed the chant as he rubbed butter into Raubel's shoulder.

There was another silence. Then suddenly, sharply—a younger Fox: "Surrender your anger! Right now! LET IT GO!" Raubel jerked like a neural patient, then began to sob. What had been troubling my friend? Had he been carrying us all?

Afterwards, passing the pipe, the wizard searched Raubel's face. "It was just an emotion," he grinned. "That's all it was." Then turned to me, as if I were next. "You can get rid of it anytime you want, Lieutenant." Then giggled.

Later, as we left, a young Jay swept our dust outside.

♦

On a warm evening in July, Captain Rausch approached me on my way to the mess and I saluted him. "Lieutenant, return to your cabin and report for dinner at 2000 hours. I have just spoken with Major Reitsch. The three of us will be dining together."

He sounded worried. The last time I'd dined with him was to celebrate his thirtieth birthday. Two hours later, they awaited me with a bottle of burgundy. I saluted and took my seat.

"Lieutenant," Rausch began, "have you heard the radio?"

I shook my head. "No, Captain, I was reading Steinbeck."

Rausch looked nervously at his superior. "*Ja*," Reitsch began awkwardly, "it seems some officers attempted to assassinate *der Führer* this morning." (Mother's prophecy! '*until that moment…*')

"Of the Wehrmacht, Major?" He nodded. "And where is this happening?"

"Wolfsschanze."

I nodded. "Ah, Rastenburg." Reitsch nodded. "Was it successful, Major?"

A private entered with our salads. Rausch brightened as his plate was placed before him. "Ah, radishes, Karl—a special treat?"

The private smiled. "Yes, Captain. Hans found them in Antelope this morning. Canadian."

"*Wunderbar.*"

Reitsch looked up. "Roast beef tonight, Karl?"

"Yes, Major."

"Tell Hans: not quite so rare , please."

"Just medium, Major?"

"If he would, please."

The private saluted and withdrew. Then softly from

Reitsch: "*Der Führer* survived, Lieutenant."

I began to sigh, then coughed to muffle it. Bud had been right: 'to the last drop.' There was a long silence as Rausch filled my glass—the stains on the tablecloth felt unbearable. "Lieutenant," Rausch continued, "one or two of your mentors might be implicated. One must expect…repercussions."

"*Ja*," added Reitsch paternally, "you must be prepared for this, Friedrich."

I thought of Colonel Einstadt, who'd insisted on accompanying me to the depot back in '41. "National Socialism is one thing," he'd told me, "Germany is another. One is an experiment, the other…the Nation." And somewhere within that bedlam, Mother was lighting matches.

"Nothing to say, Lieutenant?" Reitsch wondered.

"Nothing appears to have changed, Major."

Rausch dressed his salad. "*Ja*," he sighed, "life goes on."

Impulsively, Reitsch raised his glass. "*Auf das Leben!*" he toasted.

We all touched glasses. "*Auf das Leben!*" we chorused.

The following week the Wehrmacht adopted the Hitler salute, but Captain Collins forebade it at camp.

♦

We called it Antler University and crowned Rausch dean. To the Commandant, of course, it was just "RE"

(Recreational Education), but, as the "Democratic Ethos" track was compulsory (and thus illegal), he had reason to be subtle.

Considering how moronic classes were downstate, AU was the Heidelberg of prison scholarship. Major Reitsch taught *History of the Democratic Idea*, a philosophic survey from Ancient Greece through the Icelandic *Althing* to parliamentary hegemony in England. Collins' adjutant, Corporal Larsen, lectured on *Scandinavian Social Democracy*, focusing on the development of the Swedish Labor Party. Rausch himself held forth on *Democratic Aesthetics*, an eclectic review of Frank Lloyd Wright, the Marx Brothers, and the recent Broadway team of Rogers & Hammerstein. And I offered *Social Pluralism*, a somewhat offbeat analysis of John Stuart Mill.

Only later did we learn the program was supposed to be initiated by an Assistant Executive Officer en route from Washington. Ethos classes were supposed to be taught by UT instructors and follow the Army's curriculum.

My initial lecture was held in an enlisted men's mess. I followed the odd American practice of writing notes on cards, hoping to impress Larsen with my assimilation. After reviewing Mill's life—colonial administrator, editor, radical MP, I focused on his democratic elitism:

"Gentlemen," I began as a breeze scattered the napkins, "John Stuart Mill was a critic of every democratic government that ever ruled—indeed every democratic organization that has ever assembled. Because he believed—as many psychologists believe today—that the

104

average human being does not fully use his intellect. Only what Mill calls the 'gifted few' completely use their intellect."

The room was quiet. German students before the War had been contemptuous of what they called *die Banalität* [Banality]—the trivializing of culture in the English-speaking world. Mill became relevant in the '50s because he conceded banality while defending democracy.

I sipped some water before continuing. "'No government by democracy,' Mill says—I repeat, gentlemen, '*no* government by democracy ever did or could rise above mediocrity.' So why then is Mill a democrat?" I noticed two sergeants taking notes. "Mill admits," I went on, "that the democratic masses are a 'collective mediocrity'…The masses do not 'now take their opinions,' he writes, 'from dignitaries in Church or State, from ostensible leaders, or from books. Their thinking is done for them by men much like themselves, addressing them or speaking in their name, on the spur of the moment, through the newspapers.' Like the editorials in the *Eagle*!" I joked, and there was a peal of laughter and a smile from Larsen.

"But '*I am not complaining of all this*,' he says. I repeat this: '*I am not complaining of all this*.' In other words, he *accepts* the limitations of democracy—that is the way things are. *Ja*, he accepts them because he finds 'nothing better compatible with the present low state of the human mind.'"

The camp's collie barked at me, then abruptly left the hall. "See, it is impossible to change the mind of

105

an aristocrat!" I quipped, and my students broke into applause.

"Okay, *sehr gut*, where were we?…Collective intelligence is low and that is the way things are. So how then…how then can democratic government, er, *hinaussteigen*—"

"Rise above," Larsen coached.

"Thank you, Corporal." I sipped some water. "Yes, how may democratic government *rise above* collective mediocrity?" I retrieved Mill's essay and turned the page. "'In their best times,' Mill writes, democracies have 'let themselves be guided by the counsels and influence of a more highly gifted and instructed One or Few…The honor and glory of the average man is that he is capable of following those initiatives; that he can respond internally to wise and noble things…'

"In other words, gentlemen, democratic nations may attain greatness when their 'mediocre' citizenry 'respond internally'—*die innerliche Resonanz*—to wisdom and nobility—*auf Weisheit und, eh, Idealismus*. One may recall in this regard Pericles in ancient Athens and Thomas Jefferson here in America over a century ago…"

♦

The Manhattan Project was unknown to me, and nearly the rest of the world, until the following summer. But Bud made certain I was aware of the project by late August. I learned of the undertaking in the basement of a warehouse in Antelope. I never saw my source, who I gathered sat in an adjacent closet. We spoke over an intercom on a rainy Sunday afternoon. His code name was Pete.

"Pete," Bud began. "I'm here with Lieutenant Dassen, who was formerly a logistics man with the Afrika Korps. He's been interned over at Roberts for more than a year."

"*Guten Tag*, Lieutenant," the intercom greeted me.

I replied into the mike. "*Guten Tag*, Pete."

Bud leaned forward as well. "Pete, it might be a good idea to tell the Lieutenant just how your group came to learn about the Project."

"Sure. Lieutenant, some of our members are employed at a secret laboratory in the Southwest. Based on what they've seen and heard, they believe this facility is attempting to encase a uranium isotope in a chain-reaction explosive."

"Where is this laboratory?" I wondered. Bud was signaling his objection to my question by waving his hands.

"Lieutenant, I could be shot for revealing that."

"You could be shot for revealing the encasing!" Bud quipped.

Both men chuckled. "I'd like to avoid names and places."

"Of course, Pete. I'm sure the Lieutenant understands."

I pressed on. "Pete, is this a military laboratory?"

"Absolutely."

"Army? Air Force?"

"Army."

"I see. And how many technicians are working there?"

"Mmm…1500."

"And support staff?"

"Thousands."

"*Thousands?*" I asked incredulously. "Ten, twenty, fifty?"

The reply was cool. "Between five and ten, Lieutenant."

I clasped my hands on the table. Ten was an ominous number—the right figure for a special weapon. I grasped at a straw. "Is it possible this lab is designing atomic *engines*?"

"No, Lieutenant, it's not. This is a weapons lab and its goal is to produce a chain-reaction bomb."

"Your people are certain of this?"

There was a pause. "In the case of one of our contacts, Lieutenant, the actual assignment is to assist in the design of the casing. Now obviously—"

"*Ja, ja*, of course," I conceded. As with the Williams meeting, I began to feel anxious. "Pete, do your people know what the targets are?"

"You mean specific cities, Lieutenant?"

"No, nations."

"I imagine only Roosevelt and Churchill know that."

"It has not been discussed?"

"Not to their knowledge."

I sighed, then looked at Bud. "Okay."

"Finished?" Bud asked me. I nodded, as he leaned towards the mike. "Pete, our people at Hanford seem to be involved in producing isotopes of other elements besides uranium. Is there any talk of that in the Southwest?"

"There are apparently isotopes of other elements, yes—there's awareness of that. But the mission seems restricted to uranium."

"Good, Pete…Well, thanks for coming up. Fred and I will ring the buzzer as we leave." Bud checked his watch. "You should be clear by 1500."

"My pleasure, gentlemen. My regards to Helen, Bud."

♦

And then it was Labor Day, and Bud and I were at the rodeo in Shelburne. We each sipped Shelburne Pale as we fended off the breeze.

"Actually," Bud explained, "rodeos were a Mexican custom. The word's a corruption of the word *rodear*— Spanish for roundup. See, during roundup the Mexican hands used to show off their ridin' and ropin'. Well, after the Civil War, rodeo became an American pastime. Cowboys from the Southwest would run their cattle up the Pecos into Denver and Cheyenne."

"That's a long way," I ventured.

"Well, that's where the railway was—the ranchers would get seven or eight bucks for every head they shipped to Chicago. And those were the days of enormous spreads in Texas and Arizona—the Mill Iron in

109

Texas boasted over 150,000 acres and branded over 10,000 calves a year."

"So did the cowboys make their rodeo in the railyard?"

Bud laughed. "No, soldier, they didn't. The first rodeo was held fifty miles out of Denver." Bud called over an old rancher sitting below us. "Hey, Tom!" he shouted. "Git on up here and help me larn this greenhorn!"

Tom hobbled up the stairs…but was tall and lean, with distinguished hair. "Whaddya need, Bud?"

"Say hello to Fred here, one of those German boys we got locked up."

Tom offered his hand and I shook it. "Pleased to meet you, son."

"My pleasure," I replied.

Bud patted the bench. "Have a seat, partner." The old man sat down. "I was just tellin' Fred here 'bout that first rodeo in Deer Trail. Who won that thing?"

Tom raised the zipper on his jacket as the breeze stiffened. "A young man by the name of Gardenshire, I believe."

"Mill Iron, was he?"

"Yes, I think he was." The old man raised his index finger. "But he was riding a Hashknife."

Bud turned to me. "Hashknife was a huge spread in Arizona. This was a match between the Mill Irons, the Hashknives, and some cowpokes here on the plateau."

"When was this?" I wondered.

"Just after the Civil War," Tom answered. "They'd finished the railroad. There was a dry goods store in Denver that gave the winner a new suit."

Bud patted Tom's back. "Today he'd take home two or three grand."

I was incredulous. "Three thousand dollars for staying on a horse?"

"Oh, sure, son," Tom assured me. He turned to Bud. "Now, didn't Lou Brooks win five grand just before the War?"

"Somethin' like that," Bud agreed.

The old man pointed towards the field. "Of course, none of these boys will make that here."

Bud chuckled. "Be lucky to win five hundred, I imagine."

Tom sighed. "Well, that's wartime, I suppose." He stood up. "Now, if you'll excuse me, gentlemen, my wife is expecting some cocoa."

"Well, you give Barbara my regards," Bud told him. "Enjoy your afternoon." Tom waved, then shuffled towards the canteen.

A teenage cowboy busted out of the chute on a bronc. He was dressed in turquoise jeans and a gold vest. "Okay," Bud pointed out, "now there's no saddle on that horse but do you see the case strapped to its side? Looks like a briefcase?" I nodded. "Okay, now see the way the kid's jammin' his arm into it? That's his ridin' arm and it's gonna give him somethin' to hang on to." Within a few seconds, though, the youngster was on the ground.

I looked at my program. "This is the 'bareback'?"

Bud gulped his beer. "Jeez, the torque on that arm must be ferocious."

"It would be better with a calmer horse."

Bud shook his head. "No, that's just it, Fred. The wilder the ride, the higher your score. These kids pray for the tough one."

"Though not too contrary," intruded the Englishman sitting next to us.

Bud leaned forward to engage the stranger. "Sort of a happy medium, eh partner?"

The Brit cleared his throat. "Well, they want a bucker, that will get them their points. But they don't want a surprise—some sudden change of speed that will land them on their arse."

"Consistency," Bud smiled.

"*Rhythm*," the Brit insisted. "Riding a wild animal is an exercise in harmony. If you keep the time, Equus will tolerate you."

Later we moved to the bleachers to get a view of Team Roping. The contest requires two wranglers—a head rider to rope the steer around the horns…and a "heeler" to rope the back legs.

During intermission, four Jay Indians bobbed and sang the Chicken Dance. Eagle feathers flew from their hairpieces, which were made of porcupine quills. Eagle wings hung from their shoulders; gauntlets wrapped each forearm. They wore wool shirts with mirrors, wool leggings with hawk bells, and leather moccasins. Two drummers with clamshell breastplates squatted near the ring beating time.

Within the circle, the dancers gyred separately—sometimes stationary, sometimes threading amongst each other. Their hands and feet swayed in tandem, pausing only at angles. At times they mimicked a hen's movements—crouching, stepping, flapping their arms, then strutting with their hands on the their hips.

Bud pointed to the tallest. "That one's the master. Notice how he never stretches his arms. The Jay believe you should never display your full power—always hold somethin' back."

I can still recall the pitched chanting—coolly disciplined yet teasing chaos: *"Hey, ha, ha, hey, ha ha…"*

Bud kept tracking El Maestro. "See, he's wearing the middle feathers—from the eagle's tail." The dancer turned his back. "See 'em? White with black tip?"

"These are special?"

"Sure are. Those center ones are hard to find. I've seen 'em pay five dollars for 'em." He continued touting his favorite: "See the way he's careful not to jerk his head?" I nodded. "He's not supposed to drop those feathers. And he won't, either." The dancers returned to the rim. "Another thing you wanna watch is when the drummin' stops, how they just freeze—right on the dime."

"This is a rule?"

He nodded. "Yeah, they shouldn't be dancing beyond that last beat."

♦

We stopped by the river on our way back to camp and spread lawn chairs on a knoll. Bud had "business" to discuss.

"Fred," he began, "we need your help in protecting Germany."

Sooner or later, they were bound to draft me. "What do you have in mind?" I opened bravely.

"The American people don't want to level Germany—like you say, they're gonna need an ally in Europe to fence Stalin." I nodded. "But war is a *fever*, Fred…" A bough sped past us on its way north.

Bud sighed. "Patriots in this country…need to prove…" His voice trailed off. I looked at him expectantly. Then: "ATOMIC BOMBS MUST NOT BE DROPPED ON GERMANY!" he exploded, pounding the arm of his chair. "THIS IS MADNESS! INSANITY!" His face was red.

I held my ground. "I do not happen to think—"

"YOU'RE NOT AMERICAN!" he scolded me. "YOU DON'T UNDERSTAND THIS COUNTRY!" I looked off. He lowered his voice, but remained firm. "Towards the end of this month, there's gonna be some action here in the West. Jews-evelt is gonna learn the West will not permit—*on its own soil!*—the manufacture of weapons—"

"But, Bud—"

"– whose purpose is the annihilation of a bulwark against Bolshevism. IT SIMPLY AIN'T GONNA HAPPEN!" He took a breath. "Our group will intercept the plutonium and Washington will know why! The whole world will! And there'll be corresponding action down south."

"What is plutonium?" I wondered.

He waved impatiently. "Another metal they've extracted."

114

There must have been rockwrens chirping there but I hardly remember. What I recall was Bud's jaw and a certain *Schwäche* [enervation] I began to feel—a kind of dizziness in his presence that left me defenseless. He lowered his voice. "We're only asking you to be the lookout, Fred."

"Why me?" I protested. "You have your comrades."

My host sighed. "Fred, besides my daughter, there's simply no one else I can rely on. If Grace were alive—"

"What about your Patriots?"

He shook his head. "G-men all over the place…" His voice trailed off.

Moments passed…then silence as I fell through a singularity and emerged in another cosmos. I was now Dassen, saboteur. *Deutschland über…die Vernichtung.* [Germany transcending…Annihilation.]

I took a breath. "Okay," I conceded. "All right."

"Really? Are you with us?" I nodded. He put his hand gently on my shoulder, as I gazed across the river. It was the kind of affection I'd always dreamed of.

♦

As I jumped out of Bud's pickup, I heard Benny Goodman's "Mission to Moscow" blaring from the jukebox. It was another one of those crazy nights at Roberts—what Germans call a *Ferntrauung* [distant wedding]. This was a betrothal to a sweetheart back home—without the sweetheart, of course. (In one camp in Louisiana, she was portrayed by an impersonator…but here in sober Teton, only dolls were deployed.)

The Americans encouraged these fetes, believing them good for morale—it wasn't unusual for a camp to provide a keg for the occasion. Here in the heartland, the Swiss Consulate was also supportive, shipping *Stollen* and tobacco from Chicago. And while some officers considered these rituals silly, none considered *Stollen* a laughing matter—everyone showed up for a piece of *that*.

The feast consisted of barbecued burgers and accordian fries. Over the past year, I'd developed an appreciation for burger cuisine; along with fried chicken and the hot dog, it was surely the national dish.

As I retreated to an isolated table, I was cornered by Kurt Schultz, the troubled corporal. But tonight he was giddy with beer and news.

"*Wie geht*, Dassen?"

I switched to English to maintain my distance. "It's going well, Schultz." I sat down with my paper plate. "And how are you?"

"*Wunderbar!*" and he raised his cup to toast my health. I bit my burger. "*Ja*, Brussels fell yesterday and Bucharest the week before."

I sipped my Coke through a straw. "Yes, I noticed."

A devilish smile betrayed his sympathy. "Won't be long now!" he teased.

"This war is far from over," I warned him. (Did I need more time?)

He shrugged impudently. Then rose to leave, tipsily

crooning Crosby: "'I'll Be Home for Christmas...'"

"*Ja*, but which one?" I called out.

9

The flesh is willing, but the spirit is weak—the inverse of Christ's dilemma haunted me that week. Even before discussing Bud's plan with Helen, I felt the need to converse with myself.

I have difficulty recalling those last days of fall. A guard sold me some peyote after Labor Day and, with increasing confidence, I began to chew it in the forest. Perhaps Medicine Fox sensed it. All I can tell you is that on my next visit he spoke of me as "seeker" and encouraged me to find my "power animal."

"But which creature is it?" I implored him.

He shook his head. "I cannot guide you, Lieutenant." He pointed to the village. "My obligation is to my people."

"But I am not knowing…" My voice trailed off.

He put his hand on my shoulder. "Under the Great Spirit are Small Ones and Helping Ones," he advised me. "The Helping Ones will guide you." He pointed to the mountains.

I remember being in the shadow of Sky Peak, 2000

meters above Antelope, transfixed by the apex puncturing the cirrus. And my mustang roped to a birch, sampling the campground. And the cactus in my head, and the forest turning blue...and then, yes, Fox's beasts in the hills with mile-long snouts. And an immense lion peering down and a quivering roar echoing down the canyon.

"SABOTAGE!" it roared. "SABOTAGE OF YOUR HOSTS!"

It was a fair charge. The last incident of German sabotage had been during the previous war while a neutral U.S. was supplying the Allies. In 1915, the German consulate in Baltimore schemed to destroy munitions dumps along the East Coast, funding a German sea captain to recruit sailors and marines as operatives. Its most successful strike was in July of '16—the detonation of 2000 tons at a railyard near Jersey City.[4]

There'd been an attempt in this war as well. In June of '42, German subs deposited four agents off the Long Island coast and four off the coast of northern Florida. But within a week their leader, George John Dasch, betrayed both crews to the FBI.[5]

And there was the strange case of "The City of San Francisco," the transcontinental streamliner jointly owned by three railroads. The flyer was derailed in Ne-

[4] In 1939, an international commission found Germany guilty of sabotage within the U.S. during the First World War. The Federal Republic forked over $90 million compensation to the U.S. State Department between 1953-79. [VOB]

[5] Six were executed that August, but Dasch and a comrade were pardoned, then deported, in '48. [VOB]

vada the night of August 12, 1939. The ensuing plunge killed twenty passengers and injured sixty. The following morning the coroner ruled the wreck an act of sabotage.[6] The fact it occurred less than three weeks before Hitler attacked Poland suggests it might have been the work of German agents bent on intimidating the U.S. And although it was never solved, my instructors assumed it was an Abwehr operation.

But, if so, who were the agents? In '42 Dasch's team had been a mix of Germans and German-Americans. Was the Nevada action committed by German agents… or fascist operatives here in the West?

When one studies U.S. fascism in the '30s (as we did at War College), one learns it intensified after the recession in '37. Nazi Germany was booming, while America faltered. Yet in his Quarantine speech in late '37, FDR seemed to be drifting towards confrontation with the Axis, warning there would be "no escape through mere isolation" for an America bent on a "concerted effort to uphold laws and principles."

Cornered by the apparent dilemma of unemployment or war, pockets of urban youth became disaffected, fueling both fascist and Communist agitation. Father Mullin, an Irish priest based in Wisconsin, ranted against Jewish financiers in his weekly newspaper column. In '36, lawyer Frank Mortil founded the Liberty Alliance in Indiana, eventually adopting the swastika as the em-

---

[6] In December 1940, the now-subsumed Interstate Commerce Commission confirmed the coroner's finding. But no culprit has ever been identified. [VOB]

blem for his fascist front; its umbrella shaded George Paulson's Gold Corps, Rev. Stephen Enron's Christian Protectors, and in time, David White's Freedom Party (formerly the Gold Corps post in Spokane).

By '39, U.S. fascists were restless. The economy continued to languish, war continued to loom. In Boston, an alleged former Trotskyist, Pete O'Rourke, left Mullin's Christian Union to spearhead the Christian Vanguard, pledging action in the streets. At a Vanguard rally that July, O'Rourke threatened

> a revolution for a nationalist America—don't let anyone tell you anything different. It's a revolution against the Jew first, then against Democracy, then against the Republican and Democratic parties. Both are rotten. Both useless…We are fighting for a Christian Aryan America and you men here are part of that revolution.

The following month, a Vanguard cadre scuffled with police in Somerville, injuring two officers. At a rally there a week later, Mortil was guest of honor. He warned of Christian holy war:

> I am not content to walk in the footsteps of Christ. I will walk ahead of Him…with a club.

A week before, the train in Nevada fell into the canyon. Disgruntled mechanics? German agents? Western fascists? An informed guess would be Western fascists—not on orders from Germany but in sympathy with her. There was contact between the Liberty Alliance and Germany's Consul General in San Francisco (who the U.S. expelled in '41)…and with the Western *Bezirksleiter* [regional head] of the German-American League in LA. There was contact between an operative of the Western *Bezirksleiter* and the Freedom Party in Spokane. And the Gold Corps post in San Diego was armed and aggressive.

If German operatives derailed that train, I suspect they were U.S. fascists recruited by the League and controlled by the consulate. If fascists acted independently, my suspicion would fall on operatives recruited by Gold Corps posts in Southern California or the nascent Freedom Party.

Was this the team I was joining? The cat disappeared.

An antelope with menacing horns appeared across the canyon. *"ICH BIN DEUTSCHLAND. RETTE MICH!* [I am Germany. Save me!]" They estimated at *Abwehrschule* that an atomic bomb might kill 100,000 people within a few minutes. Should Germany be pulverized?

I reached the same conclusion Roosevelt and Churchill reached a year before. Germany must be purged of National Socialism, then revived as a democracy. I refused to believe that the culture of Leibniz, Goethe, Beethoven, and Rilke was incapable of transcending atrocity and emerging a humane force. There was too much talent—too much achievement—to warrant obliteration.

The animal withdrew.

A rattlesnake hissed on a nearby rock. "I AM ATOMIC ENERGY. REVERE ME!"

Nuclear explosions were indeed awesome…but what sort of 'reverence' was appropriate? Atomic weapons were too ruinous to be deployed. If a nation used them, they would in time be used against her, ultimately leading to suicidal warfare that would destroy the species. The only hope for humanity was to outlaw this weaponry.

Now—'44—was the time to act: to commit to disarmament, regardless of risk. "Our lives, our fortunes, and our sacred honor."

The rattler recoiled.

Moments later—or was it hours?—I was awakened by a doe licking my face. I searched its eyes. "PROTECT YOURSELF!" it cried.

Were I to assist the Patriots, my life would be in jeopardy. Even if I played a nominal role, I could be executed. Then why was I willing to gamble?

In retrospect, I see an incipient despondency had invaded me. My mission had been to impregnate Helen and I'd agreed. Yet after the pregnancy, I'd felt superfluous. I'd followed passion but emerged empty.

And so, with tacit permission, death became a solution. I'd transcended Parent and Lover. My genetic heir was anointed. I'd lived the sickle, the swastika, the stars n' stripes. What would another half century prove?

Compare this to the martyrdom I was contemplating. Whatever propaganda the Patriots might deploy, *my* manifesto would be more cogent. It would explain my sacrifice as a protest against the Bomb itself. I would live and die Atomic Hero.

The flesh is strong, the spirit is strong!

Yet the doe wouldn't return to the forest. It dogged me up the trail, then chased us down the highway. I'll never forget its cry as we broke into a gallop.

124

♦

Yes, at first it had been red and yellow, dappling hill-sides with a mongrel flame. But soon it was an orange fusion, this wanton carpet that covered Helen's patio that September.

"Must you?" I wondered, talking of sabotage as we lay in bed. The nod of her head scraped my chest. "But what of the child?"

There was a sigh. She grabbed a pillow and propped it up, then sat up impatiently. "Look, Dassen," she explained in her best Bette Davis. "You see this critter?" she asked, pointing to her belly. "It's got no future if bombs can be tossed like volleyballs. There'd be no point living in a hell like that."

I remained supine, as her hand roved below. "But couldn't Bud and I—?"

She shook her head. "*Es geht nicht.* Look, when people see a pregnant woman on the front page of the *Times*..." I grinned. "No, really, Fred, this'll be news. The American people know nothing about the designs against Germany."

"I think the American people are happy to see the destruction of Germany."

She again shook her head. "No, you're wrong, Fred, not its annihilation. Not with the Reds on the march." And as she said this she stiffened me, tactics devolving to lust. And as I entered her, I felt forever enmeshed.

♦

"Here ya go," Bud announced the next morning, handing me a seven-foot rod outside his garage. I was still drowsy. "Granger Deluxe: jasper winds, silver ferrules"—he pointed to the reel—"screw-lock seat."

It felt light. "Is it wood?"

"Tonkin bamboo. God don't grow it any tougher."

"They are making these in Teton?"

"Down in Denver before the war. Bill Phillipson's shop. Poor bastard—probably fightin' over some rock in the Pacific."

As we climbed the Antlers in Bud's truck, my guide described the flora. He pointed out his window. "That'll be the last stand of Ponderosa you'll see." I nodded. "Up ahead we'll be getting into spruce and aspen." He lunged over and pointed out my window. "Look, there's a spruce over there. See the cones?" I nodded. He chuckled. I could smell the kerosene cooking under the hood.

Later, as we hiked the creek, I was struck by the subtle greens along the bank: the pale moss on the edge, the lichens on the stones. "Now don't be studyin' the crick," he warned. "Watch the ground. There's lots you can trip on."

We stopped to scope the water; he pointed to the center. "See, you won't be seeing 'em there," he explained. "Takes too much energy to swim that fast water." Then pointed to an eddy by the bank: "Most of your trout you'll find at the edges. Oh, they'll go into the white

126

water to grab a piece of food. But they won't stay there long." He grinned. "The math don't add up."

He walked me over to the eddy. "So we'll be fishing these pools ..." Then knelt down and searched the bottom. "See that?—deep holes, places where there are lots of roots all tangled up. Those little piles are excellent spots for big fish."

Back on the rocks, we tied on my fly. "Now what's the first thing you're gonna do?" he quizzed.

"Lift the rod?"

He shook his head. "No, sir. You know, you can always tell the locals when they come here because the first thing they do is look behind 'em." He pointed to the creek. "Everybody else casts straight away"—he wheeled me around—"then spends most of the day in the willows try'na pry their flies loose." He walked me upstream. "Always look over your shoulder to see where you can cast."

You could hear Bud's heart thump once I began to sway my rod; here on the mountain, casting was an art form. He brought his arm back to demonstrate. "Come all the way back…that's right…now forward." Then shook my shoulder: "But get your whole body into it, son." He wiggled like a jitterbugger: "Your shoulder's movin', your body's swayin', your hips're swingin'." Then pointed to the reel. "Feedin' line, throwin' it back…And when you're ready to make that final cast, let the line loose—but don't crash land, that'll scare the fish!"

To my amazement I cast quite close to the eddy. "Not bad!" Bud shouted. "Now skitter back a tad." I tugged the line. "There you go…YES, SIR!…See, how that fly's floatin'—no wake behind it or nothin'. 'Cause those fish know that anythin' that's trailin' a V behind it is not something they wanna bite. Y'understand? You want a natural drift."

Ten minutes later I was setting my hook. "Keep your eyes on that fly," Bud had warned me. "As soon as it disappears, your reel'll sing—that's how you know when to set. Now, if you set too early, you'll miss 'im; if you set too late, same thing. 'Cause all the time you *have* is the time between that fish openin' and closin' its mouth."

"How am I setting the hook?"

Bud didn't skip a beat. "Rod in your right hand, line 'tween your fingers—yeah, in your left…Now as soon as he bites, what you'll do is not only give a quick tug with your left but also raise your tip with your right. The action of both these moves—"

Suddenly the fly vanished and I reflexively set the hook. And was soon contending with a six-pound rainbow.

Bud got intense. "Now, pull with your left, lift with your right…Reel in some line…One more time, son… PULL, LIFT, REEL! Who's tougher, Fred—you or that rainbow?" He tugged my rod towards him: "A bit to the right…" Then shoved it away: "A bit to the left. TIRE…HIM…OUT!"

Bud grabbed the prize as I jerked it up. Then smacked the fish on a boulder and pinned it with his hand. When the fish quit struggling, he tossed it into a creel he'd filled with grass.

Later we sipped moonshine from his Mason jar. He

sighed as he gazed at an alder bowing over the bank. "Is this the life, *Deutsch?* The windin' stream, the Antlers standin' guard…"

"The blue sky," I added.

He smiled. "You bet, soldier. That Teton sunshine."

"I think I must never go home."

He patted my shoulder gently. "We'll work somethin' out, son."

♦

By afternoon, we'd bagged a half dozen and delivered them to the Lions for their barbecue. For the nonce, we broiled a two-pounder and consumed it on the patio. There was no one else around.

He turned serious after popping a Sheridan. He lowered his voice. "Fred, E-day has been moved to the 9th." A cow mooed in the meadow.

"'E-day'?"

"The Event." Suddenly it seemed real, destined for history.

My bottle began to quiver—I quickly put it down. "Bud, I still have no idea—"

"You're on board, though?"

"*Ja.*"

He sipped more beer. "The train will be stopped downstate…at Summit."

"From Hanford?" He nodded. "Heading for the desert," I surmised. He nodded again.

"You'll drive down at sunrise with Harry Ames from Seattle."

"Western Patriots," I guessed again.

He nodded. "Harry will drive you to a lookout—nothin' dramatic, fifteen-to-twenty steps, but with a view of the tracks. There'll be a walkie-talkie inside. (Keep your gloves on when you pick up that thing.) The action will happen between 11 and noon. As soon as you spot the train, you'll relay the info—in *German*—to a field supe. He may want details. An Army Jeep will re-trieve you within ten-to-fifteen and drive you back up-state. He'll drop you at the sat' camp where some of your NCOs have been goofin' off. You'll ride back to Roberts in their pickup. No one should ask questions. If they do, there's a family up there that'll vouch for ya."

"What'll they say?"

He pinched my cheek. "That you were screwin' their daughter, loverboy! You've already got a rep!"

I looked off into the meadow. "Will Helen be okay?"

"She'll be with me—she'll be fine."

"Will I see her that week?"

"You'll get a call. She'll be at her aunt's in Granby. It's me you won't be seein'."

"How long?"

"Two or three months."

I took a breath. "Okay."

I had trouble sleeping that night—his phrases echoed in my mind. '*German* field supe'—was the Abwehr call-ing the shots? '*Army* Jeep'—were GIs involved...or had the Pats stolen surplus? When I finally dozed, I dreamt I was at the county fair riding through the Haunted House—the wheels screeching, the consuming darkness, the occasional skull.

♦

Hunting with Bud later that week:

First, the weapon, cradled like an infant: "Can't hand a rifle to a POW or they'll jail me!" he joked, leaning against his truck. Then winked: "Wait till we're in the timber."

"This is a strong gun?"

"Thirty-aught-six. Enough to drop your beast of choice." He chuckled, then stroked the receiver. "She's a champ, Fred: Weaver scope, three-way safety…"

I read the nameplate. "Winston."

"Damn straight. Only gun worth takin' up the Slope."

While riding uphill, I read Bud the pamphlet he'd given me: "*Cervus elaphus:* Rocky Mountain elk …"

"Well, your Latin's good," he chuckled. Then downshifted. "But what the rangers don't get is the elk was a prairie animal, not a mountain animal. Nowadays you've got antelope in the plains and elk in the mountains." He shrugged. "Ass backwards!"

"They are running from the people?"

"You mean the elk?" I nodded as he passed a tractor. "Yeah, that's right. Mountains are their last asylum."

We parked by a shack and hiked south. We each car-

131

ried rifles and ammo, but Bud also wore binos and a bugle. He explained the horn was actually a pipe from an old fridge: "Doesn't matter where it came from so long as it sounds like a bull." He pointed uphill. "Them bulls are possessive, Fred—their idea of a party is one bull and twenty cows. I mean, they hear competition, they're gonna come right down and root the crasher out."

About a mile in, he handed me the glasses. "Okay, take a look at the menu. See 'im cross the canyon?" I saw a blotch resting under a tree. I nodded as I returned the lenses. Bud lowered his voice. "Okay, first thing to check is the wind." He waved a blade of grass—it blew towards him. "Good. In our face. If it wasn't, he'd catch our scent and we'd be scopin' another hill. But, if ya noticed, there's also a cross breeze." He sighed. "Which we'll deal with later."

He grabbed my shoulder and dropped me to a crouch. "Hoffmans stalk secretly, son. Stay hidden—always behind some foliage or somethin'. These are alert creatures: they can see, hear, 'n' smell far better than any soldier you've ever met, so just respect that."

"How close we are going?" I whispered.

"About 300 meters." He pointed to his horn. "Then I take my solo."

We stopped at the base of the canyon and stood our rifles against a tree. Bud peered through his binos to check the game. "Siesta time. Excellent. Hasn't moved an inch." Then dropped the glasses. "Okay, I'm gonna bugle 'im in. Get 'im within 100 meters—maybe even closer. I've brought 'em so close I could throw a rock at 'em."

"You are joking me."

"Nope, they take a challenge seriously, just like I said. He'll be comin' right over." He cleared his throat, then resumed the plan: "Okay, so when I've got 'im lined up, I'll quit tootin'. That usually stumps 'em—they'll turn to catch the sound. That's the moment we set our shots."

He scoped his gun to demonstrate. "Now what you wanna do is get behind his shoulder—take out both lungs and the heart." He replaced the gun against the tree, then looked me in the eye. "This is important, Fred. Those openers gotta be clean." He pointed uphill. "You don't want the beast to suffer. And you don't wanna have to track 'im any further than you have to. I mean, a bull can put a lot of distance between you and him in a real short time—I've seen 'em go a mile with one lung shot out." He offered his hand. "So let's just drop 'im in his tracks, okay? I don't want 'im goin' five feet."

"And the cross breeze?" I reminded him, confirming the pact with a handshake.

He felt the air. "Seems to have died." Then gestured west. "Now obviously if it was blowin' forty kph, that could sway your bullet. You'd need to compensate. Same thing shootin' uphill—I'm sure they taught you that." I nodded. "At 100 meters, you're what?—a coupla centimeters higher than your sight? So you'll need to drop your barrel a tad."

I nodded. He checked his binos for the last time, then lifted his bugle. "*Viel Glück!*" he grinned. Then furrowed his brow like Satchmo in a riff…

133

10

Yet, despite it all, I evaded the umbra.

Lonely as she appears at the harbor, the Goddess has her consorts. And we Lads of Liberty embrace her twixt satin, sometimes in unison, but always with a fecund androgyny that proclaims the law. And that rule is to preserve a world in which a curious mind may articulate truths that threaten Power.

♦

I fled at the sound of danger. There was an unexpected siren in Shelburne that impelled us to seek shelter. No matter that there'd been a malfunction. It was in that basement that I suddenly—how can I explain this? What I saw were two continents—bulging South America and cavernous Africa—rushing towards one another, colliding, locking in unison. And what I felt were my hemispheres meshing. And I cannot say when I returned to the street that life seemed changed in any way. Yet for the first time in my life, I shouted my father's name.

I was dropped off at Blue Sky, a sprawling ranch a few miles from camp, and began to hoof it home. Suddenly the Packard I'd seen last summer forced me off the road. It was that stringer from the *Worker*, Lenny Hart.

He looked me in the eyes—exhausted. "Get in, Dassen. We're goin' for a ride."

I obliged, figuring he had news of Mother. "Have you been waiting all day?"

"You're not the only show in this county. I was gonna catch you tomorrow but I got lucky."

"Where are we going?"

"To a comrade's house." He turned up the radio—Crosby.

"Is it far?" He shook his head. Within a few miles we were off the blacktop. Five minutes later we reached a stone cottage, shrouded by cedars. No one was home, the door was unlocked. Hart led me to the kitchen, carrying a briefcase. He motioned me to sit, then walked over to brew Nescafe.

He took a seat after handing me my cup, then removed a large envelope. He stared at me before speaking. "Dassen," he said, "your mother's dead."

In my heart I'd known it would come—the telegram, the chat, the void. The Gestapo remained supreme—it'd just been a matter of time. I wasn't shocked, I retained composure. When one is told of death in wartime, one accepts it as a casualty.

"The Gestapo?" I guessed. (*"Mother. They* have.*"*)

He nodded, then looked off. "They hated her, Friedrich."

"Were they cruel?"

He went on as if I hadn't spoken. "She was more beloved by the rank and file than they could ever hope to be. Many of her operatives had been union. That enraged them. They also felt—" He sipped his coffee.

"How are you knowing this, Lenny?"

"The Party's got eyes and ears, Friedrich." Then raised his hands defensively. "No one they could have spared—I mean, I don't think they could've saved her." He shook his head. "Fuckin' Plötzensee." I was feeling dizzy. My messenger sighed. "The interrogators felt your mother betrayed them. Back in '39 she apparently assured them that if Germany went to war—your father won the Iron Cross?"

I shrugged. "Third Class." (What was the difference *what* she'd promised? She'd blown up factories and they'd caught her.)

"Well, she told them you were at college and she'd never betray the Reich you swore to defend."

I smiled. Mother as patriot. The *contempt* she had for them.

"There was…"—Hart swallowed—"… abuse." He pushed the envelope towards me.

I pushed it back. "Keep it, Lenny. For the Party." I tried not to sound resentful.

He nodded, as he repacked the envelope. "Uh, there's something else, Friedrich. Your uncle and aunt, Martin and, er—"

"Marie."

"Yes, er…" He looked away. "Shot in their flat."

"Why?" I demanded. "They weren't even active!" Hart shrugged—he was just the errand boy.

Driving home, he wondered if I planned to leave Germany. "I mean, post-war." It was the first time I'd heard the term.

"I don't think so," I sighed. "My field is greater developing in Germany."

"*If* Germany develops..." Did the Party want its destruction?

He let me off at the gate and I thanked him for all his trouble.

♦

I had no time to grieve—Corporal Larsen looked even paler than Hart had. He saluted me as I entered the gate. "Lieutenant, you're to report to Captain Rausch's office."

I glanced at my Batman watch. "When, Corporal?"

"Immediately...or sooner." What was *this* about?

I found Rausch pacing his office with the photos of several NCOs tacked to his wall. My salute was returned, but there was no invitation to sit.

"Where have you been, Dassen?" A different Rausch—one I dared not confide in.

"In Shelburne, Captain."

"Unaccompanied?"

"Yes, Captain."

"From now on, you are not to leave the site unescorted. That's an order from Captain Collins."

I saluted. "Is something wrong, Captain?"

Rausch leaned against the wall, then waved his hand at

me. "At ease, Lieutenant." I relaxed my stance. He took a breath. "Corporal Schultz was murdered last night."

"*Mein Gott!*" I gasped.

He pointed to the prints. "There's a couple of NCOs in Block 14 with weak alibis. Corporal Larsen is interrogating them."

"How is this happening?"

He grimaced. "Suffocation. The coroner says there was a struggle." He walked over to his desk, sat down, and shuffled through papers. "Lieutenant, I referred Corporal Schultz to you last year."

I swallowed. "Yes, Captain."

He ran his finger over an entry. "*Ja*…'referral to Lieut. Dassen, 12 September.'" He removed his glasses. "And what did the Corporal tell you?"

"He told me some NCOs were bothering him regarding information he had given the British."

"Where?"

"In Tunis. During interrogation." Surely Rausch knew this.

"What did he tell them?"

"They said he had divulged code."

He tapped his pencil. "That's treason, Lieutenant."

"But he denied it, Captain."

He swiveled towards me. "And you took him at his word?"

"Yes, of course. It sounded like the sort of silly charge the NCOs make."

"The *Nazi* NCOs," he corrected me. I nodded. He tapped his pencil again. "And what sort of punishment was contemplated?" He raised his hands. "That is, according to the corporal."

"None I was aware of, Captain."

"He was agitated, he was referred to you, but no one had threatened him?"

I nodded. "Yes, Captain—he told me he had merely been warned."

"Against what?"

"Cooperating with the Americans."

"Cooperating with the Americans?" The captain laughed out loud. "That's a little difficult to avoid in a POW camp!" I was silent. "*Nicht*, Lieutenant?"

I took a breath. "What was expected of Corporal Schultz was that he not conspicuously…"

"Ah yes, 'conspicuously.' Of course." There was sarcasm in Rausch's voice but he knew I'd given sound advice. He began leafing through a notebook. "A diary was found this morning." He gestured at it, then located a page. "It was the…er…corporal's impression you ordered him to resist the Americans." (The goddam twerp!)

"Captain!"

"Yes, Lieutenant?"

"That is most unfair."

"Why?"

"I believed what was asked of Corporal Schultz was, under the circumstances, reasonable. And I said so."

He looked me coldly in the eye. "What was asked was that he stop breathing after a pillow was pressed against his face."

I looked away. "THE ANIMALS!" I screamed. Then

140

brushed a tear. It had been a long day.

Rausch swiveled his chair and peered out the window. Then heaved a sigh. "*Ja*, the tragedy has been the humane ones have been unable to conceive of what the savages contemplate. And if one cannot *imagine* the evil…" He drifted off.

"Captain?"

He swiveled towards me with a gentler look. "Very well, Lieutenant…" He placed Schultz' notebook in an envelope. "Corporal Larsen will introduce you to your guard on Friday. I know how much you enjoy your riding."

I swallowed. "Thank you, Captain."

♦

Mother's sacrifice had to be honored and I was the surviving eulogist. Her husband was a casualty of the First War, her sister a victim of the Second. Were there a wake in Germany, the guests would risk the fate of the corpse. Even I couldn't salute her without jeopardy.

No, it'd be solitary homage at the river's fork, the Split that augurs our Creek. Toeing the sand in the spent summer, an omen of fall in the chill, I launched a toy boat I'd carved at woodshop. Sure, it was flagged, though it didn't dare fly the sickle. Just a plain red banner, like some lazy tugboat in pre-war Shanghai.

Yes, I was the boy who'd ask her to promise, to warrant the future. The hope she offered in the early '30s—

141

the Socialists and Communists would unite. Even from Sachsenhausen, the coded letters predicting a general strike. Then, when rearmament sealed prosperity, her hex on Hitler: he would overreach, the world would uproot him...

And when in '42, dismissed as naïve, she heeded her mirror, she knew what was charted: she could have integrity or life. Either survive the New Order as some blonde waiting tables...or like Artaud's gaunt saint, speak defiance in the flames. And that certain knowledge in the bath that once she left, fascism would fall: yes, the unmistakable premonition, shared with no one, that fascism rose only to snuff *her*...that only *her* breath prolonged its madness.

O Mama, it all returns...The day you took me to the Hanz plant to stiffen the union. And I, the precocious nine-year-old pinching the steering wheel off the shelf. And your instinct as the camera whined—your showmanship, Mama—to hoist me into the lens as rebel mascot. Which not only cheered those mechanics but thrilled the Rhineland.

And later, drilling my stroke in the Wannsee, waiting in the ripples as I thrashed towards your arms. And the way you cradled me when I finally arrived, crooning *Ich Bin Von Kopf* in your best alto.

When was the Depression? I never noticed, we always had money. When was fascism? I never felt the blade: the certainty you oozed shielded my neck. If I'm safe today, it's because you wouldn't brook their triumph. The whole globe felt your disdain—*Hitler* felt it and paused over the Channel, then rushed madly into Russia like a loosed parrot.

Your boat is sailing for Dakota, Mother. Into Sioux Nation where Crazy Horse wailed: "We do not want your civilization! We would live as our fathers did!" And we don't want their fascism, do we? We would live as comrades, as our fathers did.

And with that, her raft fell into the chute, destined, against the odds, for the arid Plains.

♦

Just before meeting my guard on Friday, I dropped off a pair of shoes at the repair shop. The Italian shoemaker had been transferred and replaced by a young Negro from Chicago. His name was Sam.

"From which camp are you coming?" I asked him.

He filled out my ticket. "This here's my first, Lieutenant. I only just joined the Service." Compared to the porters I'd met on the train, Sam seemed leaner, sharper.

I gestured at the garden outside. "How do you like the camp?"

"You want my opinion?"

"Yes, of course."

He placed my shoes on the shelf. "I don't think it's right for Nazi soldiers to be playin' tennis while our boys are comin' home in boxes." He turned towards me. "D'ya see my point?"

"But the men work in the fields, eight or nine

143

hours a day."

"And you officer folks?"

"Many are supervising…or teaching class."

"Let me tell you a story, Lieutenant—you seem like a thoughtful cat." I nodded. He put his hands in his pockets. "A brother in Detroit volunteered after Pearl Harbor, was trained with a tank battalion—they called themselves the Hepcaps, you may have heard of 'em." I shook my head. "Well, they ran into some trouble in Sicily and the brother lost a leg. Came home to his Mama in Memphis and was honored at a citizens luncheon, which was only right. But when he tried to take her to dinner that weekend, they wouldn't seat 'im—kept my man standing on crutches, despite the fact he had a reservation. Told him after an hour they were sorry but they'd overbooked. But then these Nazi brass from the camp come in—spur of the moment, y'understan'—with that damn swastika on the pocket same as you got, and they're seated right away. Now do you see any fairness in that?"

The tale was difficult to believe. "So they are rather serving the enemy than the wounded soldier?"

Sam nodded. "That's right, Lieutenant. Down South the *black* man is the enemy, not the Nazi." A sergeant queued behind me.

"*Ach*, this is a shame for America, this separation by the race. This is, er—" I turned to the sergeant for assistance—"*ein Makel…*"

"Blemish," he advised me.

"*Danke*, Sergeant." I faced Sam. "*Ja*, so this is a blemish on democracy down in the South."

144

Sam nodded, then handed me my ticket. "Well, folks are sayin' things are bound to change. You know, after the War."

"I am hoping so."

He waved as I left. "Those shoes'll be ready on Monday, Lieutenant. You enjoy your weekend, now."

♦

I met my guard in Larsen's office. He could've been my clone—tall, blond, mid-twenties. Larsen introduced us. "Lieutenant, this is Private Hoff. He'll be responsible for your safety."

I returned Hoff's salute. "I appreciate your help, Private."

"The private graduated from Stanford last spring," Larsen added. Then to Hoff: "The Lieutenant was fixin' to study under Professor Heidegger just before the War."

The private brightened. "Is the professor safe, Lieutenant?"

"For the moment, yes." Within two months, Heidegger would flee to a suburban castle.

Hoff trotted his mustang behind me as we made our way to the Jay. We stopped along the river to munch some cheese. Then corked our beers on a boulder.

"Have you read Heidegger's eulogy of Hölderlin?" Hoff asked excitedly. Hölderlin was a friend of Hegel's, a romantic poet. The centennial of his death had been celebrated the year before.

"You have studied philosophy, Private?"

He nodded. "You bet, Lieutenant—German idealism. Please call me Richard."

His enthusiasm was infectious. "Okay, Richard."

"Well, *did* you, Lieutenant?"

"How were you reading this tribute, Richard?"

"It was published in Germany. And then the university in Zurich mailed my department a copy."

I finally answered. "A friend wrote me about it. But, *nein*, I have not read it."

♦

It was in the sweat lodge I finally realized Fox' maturity—he was surely over 80. Like other senior heroes, he combined wrinkled skin with a remnant of tension. Yet despite his decline, his eyes were lively. Accompanying him was his apprentice, Long Tale.

The tipi was a pyramid of saplings covered with canvas. The zippered door faced the rising sun. Prior to my entrance, four steaming rocks had been placed in the pit, each angled in a different direction.

I entered nude, as instructed. Fox was deep in prayer, cupping his head with his hands. Tale was adjusting the stones with sticks.

After his prayer, the wizard lay prostrate, then silently sat up. Tale motioned to the doorway and two youths in loincloths added four more stones. A boy followed with a bucket.

Once inside, I crouched and sat on a mat. The boy sealed us in after exiting. Fox smiled at me, then sprinkled the hearth. Next he intoned his 'Removal' chant, which he translated after singing:

> Great Spirit, we call to You from Grandmother Earth. Remove us for a while from birth and death, from health and illness, from wealth and poverty, from youth and age…indeed from every distraction so we might contemplate Your power.

Then gestured towards me:

> And receive our friend from Germany, Thinking Antelope, who joins our circle today.

He had named me after hearing of my adventure below Sky Peak.

Tale lit his pipe after we were drenched in perspiration. "Indulge!" Fox coached as I inhaled the leaves. "You've been carrying a heavy bundle."

Afterwards we swam in the river, then dressed on the beach. Long Tale returned to the village to fetch Private Hoff, while Fox and I sat quietly under an elder.

It was the chemist who broke the silence. "Something is troubling you, Thinking Antelope."

I nodded. A waterfall hissed in the quiet. "I have a decision to make."

"You *had* decided. But now you consider again."

His intuition was uncanny and I longed for his counsel. But how to pose the problem? "Do you remember how you cursed the bombs, Medicine Fox?"

But he'd forgotten. "The bombs?"

I recalled his words: "Yes, the 'bombs that sweep the children off the Earth.'"

There was a flicker of recollection. "Ah, yes…"

I sucked a blade of grass. Then in harmony with the crickets: "But, Medicine Fox: there is also Tyranny!"

He held himself for warmth. "Why, yes, there is." Then raised an ominous finger: "And it is the tyrants who drop the bombs!"

"Sometimes," I countered. "But sometimes it can be the Free who drop the bombs on tyrants."

Touché—dilemma posed. The crickets paused. And then after a taut silence, Fox' reply: "There must be balance." He portrayed a scale with his palms.

"Balance?"

He looked across the river, then nodded. "We must resist the brother who would bend our step." Then gestured towards his hills: "But we must preserve our grandmother."

♦

A rematch with Captain Pechel on the first of the month, using pieces he'd bought in Shelburne. We play on the patio in the morning sunshine.

He opens provocatively—bishop to G5. Then lights his pipe. "Calais fell yesterday."

I counter with pawn to F6. "Calm down, cowboy," I warn him, pointing to the board. Then reply to the news as he plans his riposte: "The real fight starts when they cross the frontier."

He withdraws his bishop, shaking his head. "No fight, Dassen—*es ist zu Ende* [It's all over]. *Alle Schnösel* [All the twits] are applying to law school." Then chuckles.

In the end, my solitary king faced his king and pawn. Yet I was able to capture his guard and gain a draw.

11

I returned to this universe on October 2nd:

"FBI."

"I wish to speak, please, with an agent."

"This is Reilly."

"Are you FBI agent?"

"Resident Officer—that good enough? Who the hell's this?"

"My name is Lieutenant Friedrich Dassen. I am officer prisoner at the Camp Roberts. My friends are American Nazis. I have information for the FBI."

"Where are you, Lieutenant?"

"In the Camp. In a telephone cabin."

"You got somethin' you wanna warn me about?"

"Yes, Reilly."

"When's it supposed to happen?"

"9 October."

"Mmm…Lieutenant, ya ride out every day with your men?"

"*Nein*, I am not supervising POWs."

"Good. Listen carefully. After you hang up, follow your routine—play some soccer, game of chess, write some letters, whatever you do. Remain on site—*do not discuss*

151

this with anyone. Wait till I get there. Got it, Lieutenant?"

"*Ja*, Reilly."

"Good. I'll either be up tonight or in the morning."

"Where will I see you?"

"The commandant will summon you. But when ya get to his office, I'll be behind the desk. That's the way we work it."

"*Ja*, okay."

"Won't be long, Lieutenant. Get some sleep."

♦

The following morning Corporal Larsen approached me in the mess. I nearly shuddered when he looked me in the eyes. Yet he spoke casually. "Lieutenant, could you stop by the Commandant's office after breakfast?"

"Of course, Corporal." I pointed to the coffee pot. "I'll just have some coffee."

"Oh yeah, fine…Hey, how'd that match turn out with Captain Pechel?"

"Oh, we are playing to a draw."

Larsen chuckled. "Still undefeated, eh?" I nodded weakly. He checked his watch. Then officiously: "0800'll be fine, Lieutenant." He waved before leaving.

♦

Agent Reilly belonged in New York—he was short,

stocky, and retained his accent. I assumed he'd crossed some brass and got sentenced to Teton. ("The folks downtown feel you need some seasonin', Jim.") Either that or his doctor was alarmed by his cough and prescribed Dry Chinook.

The agent was quick to assure me. "Lieutenant, I want you to know no one on site knows anything about what you've told me. Captain Collins is assuming this is about Corporal Schultz."

"You know about Schultz?" Reilly nodded. "Do you know of the Western Patriots?"

It didn't ring a bell. Instead, he snatched a pen off Collins' desk and brusquely opened his pad. "Why don't you tell me, Lieutenant?"

"Well, you know of American Nazis—"

"Who are your friends, Lieutenant?"

"Bud Hoffman, his daughter Helen. A guy named Harry Ames from Seattle."

"You've met Mr. Ames?"

"Not yet."

"But you're supposed to. On the 9th." I nodded. "And where do Mr. Hoffman and his daughter live?"

I pointed out the window. "In the hills. Up in Elm."

"And you believe they belong to a group called Western Patriots." I nodded. "Have you joined this group yourself, Lieutenant?" I shook my head. "But they told you they're members."

"Well, Mr. Hoffman said he was. I assume—"

"Have they told you what their objective is?"

"*Ja*, they worry about Germany…about the Bomb."

"What bomb?"

"The chain-reaction bomb…The atomic bomb."

Reilly dropped his pen in disgust. "Lieutenant, cut it out."

"This is what they are worrying about," I protested. "They worry about Germany."

"Germany, sure. But you're tellin' me their goal is to sit here in Teton and defend *Deutschland* from chain reactions?"

I wanted to disappear, fall back in time—attend a seminar, linger in a café. "Agent Reilly," I sighed, "I am saying you the truth. Their objective is to save Germany from the Bomb."

He rubbed his face in his hands. He was tired of these *loco* ranchers and their petty crimes—smugglin' meat, dodgin' the draft, whatever. And now *this:* some cowpoke *fascisti* obsessed about bombs. Damn New York—jealous l'il trolls. 'You're gonna love the Rockies, Jim'—fuck 'em with a broom. *He* was the guy who tipped the spooks to cut the deal with Luciano! And now Lucky, Poletti, the Navy—they were *runnin'* Palermo and he could've been babysittin' Adonis back in Red Hook. Jesus!

Reilly raised his hand defensively. "Look, Lieutenant, I didn't mean to shut ya down. I, er—this is…outta my line, ya know?" He closed his pad. "Lemme make a few calls and we'll pick up after lunch, okay?" He nearly ran from the room.

For the rest of the morning, I leafed through an issue of *Chess Review* in the library. The Salvation Army had donated a couch that was surprisingly comfortable. I was intrigued by an article by Reshevsky called "Knight Moves" that included some tips on how to deploy horses in a late-game rally. "You will be very much rewarded," he wrote, "if you have protected your horsemen. They may now emerge as your pincers."

I was resisting despondency—my cursed autonomy had again isolated me. I'd lost my mother to the Gestapo, then betrayed its Fifth Column. Yet I wore a swastika, conceived a warrior, failed to protect a comrade... and now the FBI wouldn't take me seriously. Neither fascism nor socialism nor liberalism valued me—indeed, each might argue I was a threat.

My melancholy must have drawn sympathy. Over lunch, Major Einstadt walked over to shake my hand. "Lieutenant, your lecture last week was most cogent. Mill, of course, is hardly ever placed in the socialist tradition. Yet, as you indicate, his criticism of capitalism is quite profound. And although his remedy may seem naïve, well—

"I am very glad you enjoyed it, Major."

"Yes, Lieutenant, I most certainly did." He smiled. "I shall look forward to your subsequent." Then bowed like the Prussian he was. "Good afternoon." I stood and wanly saluted.

Alone and desolate, I drained my Dixie cup, as the cow across the road struggled to understand me. But like everyone else, she lacked the insight.

♦

Just before dinner, Agent Reilly stopped by the library. He seemed shaken. "Just wanna let you know, Lieutenant, Ken Harvey is driving up from Carson."

"Who is Ken Harvey?"

"He'll interrogate you. First thing tomorrow."

"You are leaving now, Agent?" He nodded. "Is Agent Harvey—"

"Major Harvey. Army intelligence." He put his hands out in front of him. "Let's just leave it like that, okay?" I nodded. "Sleep tight, Lieutenant."

♦

The next morning I expected Larsen to fetch me again. But it was the commandant who stopped by my table and invited me to his office.

Inside, he clasped his hands on his desk; his wife and children beamed from a photo behind him. "Lieutenant, you may very well be in a position at this time to assist the United States. Now, Captain Rausch has assured me—your fellow officers have assured me—that despite

156

the, er, pin on your pocket, you remain an advocate of democratic government, an officer who envisions a free Germany."

"How may I help, Captain?"

Our eyes met. "Tell the truth, Lieutenant." There was a sharp rap on his door. "Come on in, Ken," he called out. Like the commandant, Ken Harvey was tall and bronze, but well in his 70s. Collins lost no time stuffing papers in his briefcase, then rising and introducing our visitor: "Lieutenant, Retired Major Harvey." Then a gesture towards me: "Major, First Lieutenant Dassen." The commandant headed for the door. "He's all yours, podner," he muttered to Harvey.

Harvey limped to the desk, sank into the chair, then removed a gold pen from his pocket. He offered me a Camel. I shook my head—he replaced the pack. He never lit up, so I assume the tobacco was for his charges. "Lieutenant," he began, "I want to apologize—and I genuinely mean this—for Agent Reilly's response."

"He does not seem to understand the Bomb."

There was terror in his eyes, as if my knowledge of the Bomb was America's nightmare. He rolled a pencil across the desk, straining to appear unperturbed. "Well, it's not his job really," he remarked nonchalantly. Then shrugged: "FBI. You know."

I know??? Overnight I'd gone from nutcase to confidant.

Instantly I took charge, later marveling how I dared bark orders to a superior. To begin with, his age rankled me: National Socialism was young—youth was required to strangle it. NOW. TODAY. And I suddenly needed fascism snuffed—the rage was finally welling: *die Hitlerjugend* (how dare they?), *die Heeresschule* (boring!), conscription (goodby, Heidegger!), genocide (the ghouls!), Mother's mutilation, Schultz' suffocation. There was no longer room on this planet for both Dassen and fascism.

"Major Harvey, the Western Patriots try to stop a train on the 9th. You must prevent them."

He began jotting furiously. "Where?"

"Somewhere near Summit. 'Downstate,'" I mimicked.

"Did they tell you where it's headin'?"

"Some lab in the desert. In the Southwest maybe."

He looked up. "Call me Ken. Let's get this thing over with."

I nodded. "Call me Fred."

"Fine. At what time will they intercept?"

"In the morning. Around noon."

"Who's involved?"

"Bud Hoffman; his daughter, Helen; this guy from Seattle who I never meet, Harry Ames—"

"Yeah, we know Ames." He met my eyes again. "And yourself, right?" I nodded. He returned to his pad. "Explosives?"

I shrugged. "Maybe. Derailment. They are not saying to me."

"Look, we want you there. The train'll be empty, it'll be a dummy, nothin'll be at stake. But you ride down with Ames, take your post, follow orders."

"But no violence, Ken," I insisted. "No shooting."

He stretched out his hand and I clasped it. He shook his head innocently. "No, that's right, son. No shooting."

I looked down. The Major tapped his pencil. "Helen carries my child."

He heaved a sigh. "I'm sorry, Fred." His eyes glazed. "Fred, I'm just—"

I raised my hand. "No, please you should not understand me wrong." My English was collapsing—I was sounding like some NCO. "Helen and me—it's not the man, the wife. She has the baby, then I am returning to Germany."

The Major strained to be sympathetic. "Yeah…lotta gals in Europe goin' that route…Wartime…Well, you're a handsome fella…"

I looked down. "*Ja.*"

"She'll do time," he added softly. "If it's a dummy train, with a bunch of cows, it shouldn't amount to much—coupla years…her Dad's the mastermind, so if she cooperates…"

I snickered. "Helen is not betraying Bud. This is not happening."

Harvey nodded. "Two-to-five. She'll be out in eighteen months."

A jeep passed by the window. "Just no shooting," I repeated.

The major looked me in the eyes. "Uncle Sam says no shooting."

I took a deep breath. "Okay, Ken."

He stood up. "Now, I need a couple of favors from you."

I was too exhausted to stand and salute. I stared at my boots. "*Ja*, okay."

"You'll never see me again. There's no Ken, no Harvey, I'm not Army intelligence."

"Who are you?"

He raised his voice. "Not important. And another thing: once your Pats are in custody, not a word about this chain-reaction bullshit. Not that you'll have opportunity."

A flash of indignation. "Do you send me to prison too?"

"Nope—you're in the circle now. If your warning proves out, you'll be welcome to settle here after the war."

I was touched. "Thank you, Major."

"But while the Goose steps, you're in confinement. Figure—what?—another year or two?"

"Solitary?"

"I don't think so. But you won't be ridin' any more donkeys to pow-wows." I smiled. He stretched out his hand. "Whaddya say, Lieutenant?"

I felt compelled to return to the Bomb. "Major, there is coming a day when the chain reaction—"

Again, the panic...then his hand on my arm: "Lieutenant, look, if some damn fool sets off a reaction somewhere, well, fine—you go yap about it. Sign a petition, for all I care." Then the Lie: "We're just concerned about worryin' folks. You're a teacher. I'm sure you understand."

I nodded. We shook hands.

♦

October 4th through 8th—the most absurd days of my life. Bud, Helen, and I had agreed to avoid each other a week before E-day. On the 9th, Ames would retrieve me a mile from camp.

Although I didn't realize it, this was my transition—from fascism to liberalism, from war to peace, from Germany to the world. I pledged no allegiance to Hitler, Stalin, or Roosevelt—like all true liberals, I was only loyal to reason.

But sitting comfortably in maturity, you can't imagine how lonely it feels when the infant takes that step—the fear of falling, injury, suicide. As in Nietzsche:

> *Der Mensch ist ein Seil, geknüpft zwischen Thier und Über-mensch—ein Seil über einem Abgrunde. Ein gefährliches Hinüber, ein gefähr-liches Auf-dem-Wege, ein gefährliches Zurückblicken, ein gefährliches Schaudern und Stehenbleiben.*

> [Man is a rope stretched between the animal and Over-man—a rope over an abyss. A dangerous crossing, a dangerous wayfaring, a dangerous looking-back, a dangerous trembling and halting.]

But in the end it wasn't Nietzsche I read. I rummaged through a box of books the Kiwanis had donated. I found a copy of *Wagoner's Diary*, the journal of a German teamster, who settled in Ohio in the 1840s. The notebook was plainly written, yet contained a poignant description of liberty:

> Most men imagine, they are servants to a plenitude of masters—their Deity, their Savior, their tribe, their ruler. I

161

leave to philosophers to determine whether such obedience is natural and, if so, whether it derives from deficiency. But what may be said of America is that she does not require such service. As a man deems appropriate, he may volunteer his piety, his loyalty, his schooling, his valor, to beings terrestrial or otherwise. But as an American he is not compelled to do so.

♦

Harry Ames was Canadian, born in Calgary at the turn of the century. He spoke that Albertan English the guards liked to call 'Scotch Canuck.' He was slim and dour with a nondescript face. To be honest, I hardly remember him.

We didn't talk much—certainly not about politics. I could only imagine that, like Bud, he was hysterical about the Russians and horrified at Germany's demise. He occasionally betrayed his views. I remember him saying something like, "Well, as soon as this one's over, the next one starts straight away, 'ey?" I assumed he meant the West would be battling the Soviets the day Berlin fell. (I thought of him during the Cuban Crisis.)

He was a great fan of Helen's. "Isn't she a sweetheart?" he asked with a thin smile. "You're a lucky one, you are." He seemed to think she was a brilliant intellectual. Helen was bright, with good instincts, but in no way theoretical. But Harry saw genius.

Sunrise was spectacular—rays leaping over the buttes. But not quite Homeric—they were ribbons, not 'fingers'—crimson, not 'rosy.'

It occurred to me this jaunt was my Teton Farewell. As part of democracy indoctrination, officers were being segregated in separate camps. And Harvey had warned me I'd be specially detained. So it was unlikely I'd return to Roberts—I was probably destined for some shack in the desert.

We stopped at some tables near Caveman for what proved to be my only meal. It was hardly special—Wonder bread, potato chips, American cheese (the worst curd in the world). Harry had iced a case of Nehi, a popular grape drink at the time. (America and its wartime pop—Yoo-Hoo, Nehi, Squirt.)

Somewhere west of Summit, we veered up a path. Twice in the past month I'd been driven up hidden lanes—have never allowed it since. In the '70s I felt for Hoffa when his godson took him for a ride. ["Hey, Chuckie, where the hell ya goin'? Take the goddam freeway, noodlehead."—VOB]

As we climbed, I caught a glimpse of the tracks. Then spotted a newly-erected tower a mile above the highway. Ames pulled beside it, then killed the ignition. "All right, soldier, you know the drill." He offered his hand and I shook it. "G'luck, Lieutenant." He managed a grin.

As I climbed the ladder, Ames headed downhill. I felt completely absurd on that rung. I'd forgotten everything—why Germany was Nazi, why I was an officer, why I was in America, why we were stopping the train. But like a good German, I followed orders.

My mood changed when I reached the cabin—the forest renewed my purpose. The cedars stood proud in the

163

sun. I suddenly realized this was history's first protest against the Bomb. I put on my gloves and reached for the binos. Then checked Batman. It was 9:20.

Two hours later, I sighted a train—a steam engine with a string of cattle cars. I searched for the caboose, hidden in the trees. Then suddenly: gunshots. The train creaked to a halt. Were the Pats firing? Two police cars screeched up to the tracks. Then more gunfire.

NO, STOP!

I heard a cop over a loudspeaker: "THERE ARE ONLY CATTLE ON THIS TRAIN. I REPEAT: THERE ARE ONLY CATTLE ON THIS TRAIN." An ambulance pulled up to the tracks. Orderlies jumped out, removed stretchers from the rear, ran into the woods.

Then it dawned on me: HELEN! THE WARRIOR! MY GOD!

I remember running down the path, sobbing to myself: *Was hab' ich getan? Gott hilf mir, was hab' ich getan? Oh Gott, was hab' ich nur getan?* [What've I done? God help me, what've I done? Oh God, what've I actually done?]"

When I reached the tracks, they were tossing corpses into a truck. The bodies were zippered. Helen was on a stretcher, with a wound in her chest. There was no sign of Reilly or Harvey.

The next thing I know I was in handcuffs. "THIS IS MY WIFE!" I screamed. "YOU MUST ALLOW ME! I HAVE RIGHT TO VISIT MY WIFE!" They walked me to her stretcher while they readied transport.

She grinned drunkenly when she saw me. She stretched

out her arm: "*HEIL* HITLER, FREDDIE!"

"No, baby, *ruhig bleiben*…[stay calm…]"

There was a glint in her eye—but how could that be? "*DEUTSCHLAND*…," she mumbled. But was failing.

OH, GOD!

I remember the hatch closing and the sign on the door: Coal County Clinic. In pale blue script.

"ASSASSINS!" I screamed, as the ambulance left. "IMPERIALIST SWINE!" Instantly my legs were shackled and I was thrown into a patrol car. They weren't careful—my shoulder smashed into the door.

The cops were silent on the road. "*Was habe ich nur getan?*" I kept sobbing. We made our way to some army base. It began to rain. There was a sharp pain in my elbow.

Dassen had broken through. Existence was now alone.

Part Two

Autumn 1944

It was a private hospital room, with pale walls and venetian blinds. The view from my window was Endless Prairie Sliced by Two-lane Blacktop. It was late morning and I was still drowsy. I assumed I'd been sedated. After lunch, a plump nurse visited me. "Lieutenant Dassen, I'm Nurse Peterson. Do you know where you are?"

"The prairie?"

"Well, that's right, Lieutenant—you're in Crosby Hospital, the largest Army hospital in the world. We're in Camp Crosby, about fifteen miles south of Colorado Springs." She smiled. "Actually, the prairie meets the Rockies here—when the weather's clear, you can see Pike's Peak."

"The building, it's new?"

"We opened two years ago."

I propped myself with a pillow. "Why am I sick?"

"I'm going to let Dr. Rosen explain that to you. She'll be coming by at 4:30."

"This is Tuesday?"

"No, Lieutenant, it's actually Wednesday, October 11th…Okay?" I nodded. "Your wristwatch is on the table. I've set a radio for you on the shelf." She pointed to the night table. "Do you see it over there?"

I leaned forward to check. "*Danke schön*," I smiled. I was receiving privileged treatment.

"I'm leaving the *Gazette* on the chair. If you need any-

169

thing else, just buzz. They'll be wheeling in dinner after the doctor sees you."

Dr. Rosen stopped by before five. She reminded me of the Jewish women Mother used to conspire with—tall, angular, intense. She wore no uniform—in fact, she was fashionably dressed.

She pulled up a metal chair. "Good afternoon, Lieutenant, I'm Dr. Rosen." She had a New York accent.

"Good afternoon," I nodded. "You will tell me, please, why I am sick."

She nodded. "Well…you became upset Monday when two officers sought to drive you to safety. You had to be sedated." I nodded. She removed a pad from her briefcase and began to take notes. "Do you remember the interception of the train, Lieutenant?"

"Sure I am remembering," I snapped. "Does my wife live? Does our child live?"

"I have no information about that, Lieutenant."

My anger returned. "But I must know this!' I demanded. "I have right to know this!"

She shook her head. "Information about the incident is classified, Lieutenant. I'm sorry. They wouldn't tell me if I asked."

I crossed my arms. "I will not speak unless they are telling me if my wife and child live."

Rosen ignored me—she'd dealt with ultimatums before. "Where were you when the train was stopped?" she pressed on. I looked defiantly out the window. "Lieutenant?" I wouldn't face her. Her voice sharpened. "Lieutenant, I'll be unable to discharge you if you refuse to cooperate."

I studied the flatland in my window. There was a despondency on the prairie we'd escaped in Teton. I longed for Sky Peak.

She snapped her pad and packed her case. "Very well, Lieutenant. Have it your way."

♦

I awoke the next morning to find some guy reading the paper in a chair beside my bed. "Who are you?" I asked nervously.

He put the paper down. "Name's Gene Killus. I'm here to talk some sense into you." He was slick, urbane—nothing like Harvey.

I sighed—things kept getting more complicated. "May I use the toilet before?" I asked.

He rose and headed for the door. "Take a half hour, Lieutenant—clean yourself up. I'll get some coffee. You like cream?"

"Just black, please."

He returned in twenty minutes with a nurse carrying a tray. She set the cups on the table. "Good morning, Lieutenant," she greeted me. Then exited.

I was propped in bed. Killus brought my cup to the night table, then retrieved the other and sat in the armchair. He took a sip, then placed his cup on the table. He relished the flavor. "Mmm, better than the crap they were brewing last spring." I smiled. My Angus mooed in the pasture. "So what's this bullshit you're not talkin' to the shrink?"

"Dr. Rosen is psychiatrist?"

"Yeah, from DC. Why the hell aren't ya cooperatin'?"

I folded my arms. "I am not crazy."

"Great, and I'm not Goebbels. Who gives a fuck?" I looked out the window. "Listen, *Dummkopf*, you're an enemy combatant and you've conspired against the United States. Would you rather be executed?—believe me, that can be arranged!"

I furrowed my brow. "I am FBI informer. Major Harvey promises I become U.S. citizen if my warning is true."

"Major who?"

"Harvey. Ken Harvey."

"Well, I don't know what the Army told you, or who the hell this Harvey is, but my orders are—"

"To kill me?"

He raised his hands. "Hey, back off, Lieutenant—give me some room, huh?" I reached for my cup—it was clear I wasn't getting breakfast until I satisfied my visitor. He sighed. "Look, the Army made you a promise, I'm sure they're gonna keep it—this ain't Germany. But you've gotta hold up your end." I nodded. "We don't want attention drawn to this thing. We don't want contact between you and that group. *Anyone* in that group! Do yourself a favor, Lieutenant—forget 'em, huh?"

"You are not Army?" He shook his head. "Then who are you?"

"Don't worry who I am. Worry 'bout keepin' your ass

outta the Chair, okay?"

"Does my wife live? Does my child live?"

He waved me away. "We'll get to that…Now, Dr. Rosen's your therapist—you *work* with her. You're an only child, you never knew your father—she'll probably find you fell under the influence of those loonies. That'll give us an alibi and you'll walk."

"Walk where?"

Killus chuckled. "Slang expression, Lieutenant. Means you'll go free."

"But she asks about the plan."

"That's okay—she's got clearance. Tell her the truth—she'll take it to her grave."

I was beginning to see their strategy. "And my wife?"

"Miss Hoffman ain't your wife, Lieutenant."

"She carries my child."

He sipped some coffee, then looked me in the eyes. "Look, her father—that madman—what's his name?"

"Bud."

"Yeah, Bud. They plugged him full of holes."

"MAJOR HARVEY PROMISED NO SHOOTING! HE SHOOK MY HAND!"

"I never heard of this guy!"

"HE PROMISED ME!"

Killus raised his palms again. "Okay, hold your horses!" He reached for his cup and gulped more brew.

I put my head in my hands. "Oh, *mein Gott*," I moaned, *"was haben ich getan?"*

"Lieutenant?" he prodded. I looked up. He lowered his voice. "Look, Lieutenant: d'ya think the cops *wanted* gunfire?"

I sampled some coffee—tried to be reasonable. "I suppose they are wishing no corpse."

"Corpses? Fuck!—they didn't want the *noise*, Lieutenant! They didn't want anyone to know!" I nodded. "Now, the press knows *nada* about any of this and, with your help, maybe it can stay that way.

"I gave my word, Mr. Killus. I am German officer."

"Well, good, we're makin' progress…Now your man Bud resisted arrest. I'm sorry but the cops weren't about to let a saboteur go back to his ranch during wartime. Back in '41, we lost some engineers."

"And Helen?"

He looked out the window. "She's alive, but…"

"She will die."

He sighed, then faced me. "I don't think…" He grimaced. "She's not going to make it."

I threw off my blanket. "You must permit me to see her!"

He rushed to the bed and pinned my arms. *"Blödmann* [Asshole], you're goin' nowhere! Don't be an idiot!"

I began to sob—he released me. "You are killing her!" I shouted. Then louder: "MURDERER!"

He was losing patience. "Friedrich, dammit, you go to her deathbed—swearin' you love 'er—you're signin' your death warrant, can't you see that?"

"You kill her, then you kill me."

"NO! YOU'RE AN ACCESSORY, FRIEDRICH! WE'RE TRYNA SAVE YOUR ASS! GIVE US A BREAK!"

I reached for a Kleenex and blew my nose. He stood

up—the crisis had peaked and he knew it. "Let her go," he said quietly. "You lost your Mother, those creeps took advantage…You're no Nazi, son, we know that."

I sniffled. "*Ja*, I am social democrat."

"You're a bright fella with your whole life in front of ya. Christ, what I wouldn't give to be twenty-five."

They wheeled in a cheese omelet after Killus left. By some miracle, the cheese was Swiss.

That afternoon Dr. Rosen returned, sporting a turquoise blouse. "Should we try again, Lieutenant?"

I motioned her to sit down, then gulped. "I wish to apologize you for the rude way I am behaving."

"Lieutenant, tomorrow you'll be moved to your own cottage. You'll find your belongings from Roberts were carefully packed. Unlike Roberts however, you'll be continually guarded, so you'll need to adjust to that. But I'd like you to visit me at 3:00—I'll give you my office number." She removed a pad from her purse, jotted down some figures, then handed me the note.

I stuffed it in my pajamas. "But you are accepting the apology?"

"Of course I am." She placed her hand on mine. Then softly: "Friedrich, I want you to know we're all very much aware of the awful manner in which you lost your mother—we're deeply sympathetic." I nodded. "And the courage you displayed in reporting the Hoffmans—" she swallowed—"that was brave."

I looked away—my eyes were glassy. "*Sehr gut*, doctor. I see you tomorrow."

She removed her hand and stood up. "I'm very much

looking forward to it. Sleep well, Lieutenant."

For the next three weeks, I was confined to hospital grounds—its gym, cafeteria, library. Separated from physics and philosophy, I threw myself into the study of oncology and stood before the Metastatic Sphinx pondering the malignant riddle.

As for therapy, I submitted to sixteen sessions that Dr. Rosen recorded on her Armour.[7] Just before her death in '89, she mailed me a transcript of the sessions. I've appended excerpts from nine:

10/13/44

    R: You know what day it is, Friedrich?

    D: Friday.

    R: And the date?

    D: 13 October...*Ach so*, Friday the 13th!

    R: Are you superstitious?

    D: What means this?

    R: *Aberglaubisch*.

    D: *Ach so*. Well, man say the day is not lucky.

    R: Well, hopefully, the roof won't cave in...Tell me, Friedrich: your mother never remarried?

    D: No.

    R: Were there lovers in her life?

    D: I did not know any.

    R: She was interned in '33?

    D: (nods)

---

[7] Although Armour wire recorders were not commercially available until 1946, Model 50 was issued to select units during the War. [VOB]

R: You were thirteen?

D: Almost.

R: Mmm…Is it fair to say you were the most exciting male in her life?

D: I was a lad only.

R: Did you find your mother attractive?

D: *Nein*, nothing special. There was the Blue Angel.

R: Oh, right, Marlene Dietrich—what was it you liked about *her*?

D: Er, her far-ness.

R: Her 'far-ness'? You mean her distance from other people?

D: *Ja*.

R: Right…'I vant to be alone.'…Friedrich, was your mother attracted to you?

D: There was nothing among us.

R: Of course not. But do you think she was attracted to you?

D: There was not like this talk even.

R: No attraction at all…

D: Father was dead, I was single child, she was adoring me…

R: Of course. As any mother would.

D: Yes, just like mother and son.

10/16/44

R: Your mother was a Communist, Friedrich?

D: (nods)

R: A Party member?

D: After Stalin is signing the Pact with Hitler, she is

burning the card in the chimney.

R: But she joined the Underground…

D: *Ja*, the Underground is not Communist only.

R: I understand. Are you a Communist, Friedrich?

D: *Nein.*

R: Nor a Nazi.

D: No.

R: What *are* your views?

D: Well, I like the freedom they are having here—the freedom to speak and write. But the very rich people and still the poor people—the Negro people in the South, the Indian people here in West…the broken houses they are having to live in…

R: But you favor democracy.

D: *Ja, ja*, democracy. But a parliament that is serving Capital as *ein Kammerdiener* [a valet]—this is not right.

R: You know, I have a book for you—a friend mailed it last week. It's called *Socialism of our Time*.

D: Thank you.

R: Do you know who Norman Thomas is?

D: Normann *Toe*-mass…*Ja*, we read in Germany, he tries for President, he is against America fighting the war.

R: Well, he's had second thoughts about *that*. But he's a socialist and a democrat. As I think you are.

D: *Ja*, social democrat…Thank you. I will read this.

10/19/44

D: Now I would like to ask to *you* questions.

R: Shoot.

D: Are you Jewish?

R: Yep. Is that okay?

D: Yes, of course. I was curious only.

R: Did you associate with Jews when you grew up?

D: Of course. When I was in Obserschule, there were 150,000 Jews in Berlin.

R: Hmm, nearly ten percent of the city…You met them at school?

D: Sometimes. But when I was child also, leaders of the Party would visit.

R: They were Jewish?

D: Some.

R: Like who?

D: Oh, I am thinking…Rosa Levine, Ruth Fischer…

R: Did you have any Jewish friends?

D: No.

R: Did you avoid Jewish students?

D: I had friends—it is happening they are not Jewish. 'Is that okay?'

R: Sure…Last year Nazi propaganda boasted there were no Jews left in Germany.

D: *Ja*, many have left.

R: And been murdered.

D: There are reports…

R: Do you doubt them?

D: I am not the number sure but…

R: Well, prepare yourself, Friedrich. Because after Berlin falls, we're going to find out. Not only in Germany but throughout Europe. And it may be several million.

179

D: *Mein Gott!*
R: Prepare yourself.

10/23/44

R: Are you in love with Helen?
D: She was mother to my child.
R: Mr. Killus told you she's dead?
D: He said she soon dies.
R: But are you in love with her?
D: Not actually.
R: A wartime romance…convenient for both.
D: *Nein*, more than convenience.
R: But not love.
D: *Nein…Anhänglichkeit.*
R: Attachment.
D: Yes, attachment only.
R: But the relationship was sexual.
D: *Ja*, sexual, sure.
R: Would you have married her after the war?
D: *Nein*, she is not wanting this.
R: She wanted to bear your child but not marry you.
D: Yes, I am returning to Germany, she is staying in Teton.
R: This was her wish.
D: (nods)
R: Did she have another boyfriend?
D: No.
R: Who would help rear the child?
D: Rear?
R: Yes, bring up the child…*erziehen.*

D: *Ach so.* Her father.

R: Ah, yes, the father—Bud, right?

D: (nods)

R: She lived with him?

D: Yes.

R: They were close.

D: *Ja*, close. They were *die Genossen* [comrades].

R: You mean politically—as fascists?

D: As fascists, as ranchers, as Hoffman family.

R: Was there a sexual relationship between Bud and Helen?

D: You are asking always about sex between the parent and the child!

R: Yes, and I'll tell you why. People tend to be attracted as adults to the pattern to which they were conditioned as children.

D: You are believing I made sex with my mother? *Ach,* this psychology is *der Wahnsinn* [lunacy]!

R: You don't think your relationship with your mother was unnaturally close?

D: *Nein!* And Bud and Helen were not either making sex.

R: You don't think their relationship was close?

D: Well...maybe a little odd. But not *pervers.*

10/25/44

R: Whose idea was the interception of the train?

D: They were not telling me.

R: It was planned by the group?

D: Yes. Or the Abwehr maybe.

181

R: Who involved you—Bud or Helen?

D: Bud.

R: Did you know Helen would participate?

D: Yes.

R: Did she encourage you to participate?

D: She is demanding I talk with Bud.

R: Did he threaten you?

D: No, he is asking only.

R: Yes, and at first, you agree. Then you have second thoughts.

D: (nods)

R: But you don't tell him about your misgivings. You go to the FBI.

D: (nods)

R: Did you like Bud?

D: Yes, he is teaching me about the land.

R: About ranching?

D: About rodeos, riding…hunting, fishing…the Indian people.

R: About fascism? Did he teach you about fascism?

D: He was one time speaking of race, of the Aryan.

R: Were you persuaded?

D: Not really. I believe each race has talent that it is sharing. But not…

R: To dominate?

D: *Ja*, not to oversee the others.

R: Or exterminate them.

D: Of course not.

10/27/44

R: After you agreed to help the Patriots, you learned of your mother's murder.

D: Yes.

R: Were you shocked?

D: No. Soon or late, the Gestapo finds always its enemies.

R: Her arrest was inevitable.

D: (nods)

R: Were you angry?

D: I feel the Communists are using her.

R: You felt she was exploited.

D: *Ja*, they are asking so much. She was labor organizer—okay, the Nazis send her to Sachsenhausen. She by some miracle goes free. And then the Underground—very dangerous. She by this time is serving five years in the camp. She gives twenty years—enough!

R: 'I gave at the office!'

D: What is this?

R: An expression we have in America. When a charity comes to your home and knocks on the door for a donation, you tell them: "I'm awfully sorry, but I already gave my donation at the office."

D: *Ja*, same thing! Mother gave already at Sachsenhausen! It was enough, *nicht?*

R: Were you angry at the Gestapo?

D: The Gestapo is primitive animal…It is hard to hate it—it is more like…*Verachtung*.

R: Contempt.

D: *Ja*, civilized people—we are above these beasts.

10/30/44

R: You were aware that intercepting a shipment was illegal?

D: Yes.

R: And you were aware that intercepting a military shipment during wartime was sabotage.

D: Yes.

R: Then, Friedrich: as a ward of this country—receiving humane treatment, as an opponent of fascism, with your own mother risking her life…how could you agree to it?

D: But I am never agreeing to stopping the shipment.

R: You agreed to be sentry.

D: Yes.

R: Why?

D: I am told America was making secret project to build a bomb.

R: Told by who? Bud?

D: First, yes. Then he is introducing me to engineers.

R: You *believed* them? How did you know they weren't fascists posing as engineers?

D: Posing?

R: Pretending. *Vortäuschen.*

D: They are not pretending—they are engineers knowing the project.

R: Are you qualified to recognize one?

D: Yes.

R: Really? What are your qualifications, Friedrich?

D: I am training as logistics analyst. I study also spying at *die Abwehrschule.*

R: All right, for the sake of argument, let's suppose the U.S. is producing a bomb. Why sabotage the train?

D: Bud is telling me the train will carry fuel for the Bomb.

R: Again—did you believe him?

D: Yes.

R: Was this verified as well?

D: No, I am trusting Bud on this.

R: But as an opponent of fascism, why would you *sabotage* the project?

D: One is making the weapon, one is using it—this is the history lesson. The atomic bomb will destroy Germany, then Japan, then Russia, and, *ja*, even the U.S. finally. It is the world going along with its death.

R: If the U.S. is researching a bomb, it's because it fears Germany obtaining it first. It seeks deterrence.

D: There is of this no chance.

D: Deterrence?

R: *Nein*, I mean there is no chance Germany will first make it. America is ahead far of Germany.

R: But German propaganda speaks of a secret weapon…

D: Germany will not beat America on this.

R: And you're certain that once America obtains the Bomb, it will drop it on Germany and Japan.

D: If Germany or Japan to the last blood is fighting, America will drop the Bomb on who resists her.

11/3/44

R: But you must take responsibility for who you are

185

and what you do.

D: I do this.

R: You know, responsibility requires knowledge—
self-knowledge.

D: I know what I am.

R: Do you want to know what I see?

D: (nods)

R: I see Helga as a doting mother and your resentment of her during adolescence—the constraint this intimacy imposes. But *repressed* resentment because of your own outrage at National Socialism and admiration for your mother's struggle against it.

D: What means 'repressed'?

R: *Verdrängt.*

D: *Ach so.*

R: The repression depletes your energy, drains your libido—which leads to your isolation, your celibacy… your penchant for metaphysics, which is compelling because it offers escape from the 'dimensional world,' as you put it.

D: This is quite a story!

R: I see Bud as the father you never had—the fishing, the hunting, the rodeo—the father you always longed for. Subconsciously *(unterbewußt, ja?)*, fascism offers you the Risen Father from the First War—the Wehrmacht, the Iron Cross—while communism remains the Suffocating Mother. It's absolutely no surprise to me your first sexual relationship (and paternity, for that matter) would be realized in a fascist context.

D: But I was arguing with Bud always!

R: Let me finish. I view the Patriots' concern with the Bomb as opportunism—a ploy to mobilize opinion against the denazification of Germany. The fact that their call resonated with you—well, here again, I think it offered a noble way for you to bond with the virile Father and reject the feckless Mother.

Metaphysics offered you prestigious escape from reality. Disarmament, if that's what it is, offered you respectable alliance with fascism.

D: But I betrayed the Patriots!

R: Yes, you did…but only because the mutilation of your mother revived guilt about your resentment of her. In the end, it was more comfortable to relieve your old guilt than celebrate your new virility. Through her agonizing death, Helga finally got to you. She trumped Bud.

D: But you are glad I betrayed the Patriots.

R: As an officer, as a Jew, I can't condone fascism, no—no matter how it energizes you. As a psychiatrist, well…I look forward to the day when you can libidinally function in a democratic society. After all, there are liable to be quite a few now.

D: Democracies?

R: Yes.

D: I am hoping so.

11/6/44

D: You are not believing there is an atomic bomb?

R: Oh, I suppose there eventually might be. After the war.

D: You are not believing America will drop her Bomb on who resists her?

R: You mean in this war?

D: Yes.

R: Assuming a Bomb is developed, no, I don't expect America to use it. America doesn't *need* to annihilate civilians—the U.S. is perfectly capable of conquering humanely, as you well know.

D: (nods)

R: Well, Friedrich, this concludes your therapy. This is our final session—I'm returning to Washington on Monday.

D: Thank you, Dr. Rosen, for how you help me.

R: Well, thank *you*, Friedrich, for being receptive to therapy—I think you've made substantial progress. I'm phoning the PMG [Office of the Provost Marshal General] this afternoon and assuring them you pose no threat to security and may be reassigned. You understand they've now segregated officers from enlistees, so you won't be returning to Roberts.

D: Yes.

R: There remains the matter of the indictment against the Patriots. My understanding is you haven't been charged nor will you be, providing, of course, you sever your relationship and testify against them when requested.

D: Testify against who?

R: Apparently some survived. You will, of course, cooperate with the U.S. Attorney.

D: *Ja*, of course.

R: Good. Well, good luck to you, Friedrich. I hope things go well for you in Germany.

D: Thank you, Dr. Rosen. I say also my best wish.

Part Three

November 1992

Berkeley mirrored each decade after the war. In the '50s, you could walk down to Albany and catch Thelonius Monk at the Underground. Or dispute *Sisyphus* with the beats at Café Med'. In the '60s Savio was holding forth and you could throw your 'body on the gears' and stop the Machine. The '70s came early—by '69, Reagan's whirlybirds were buzzing the Faculty Club. Come the '80s and the Yippies were Yuppies and the kid who sold you speed was marketing software for your Gameboy. (Walk along the bay and the Titans of Tech moor the landfill: Innovative Networks, Cybernetic Interface, Regional Robotics…)

Four months after Perot, Clinton was elected. Conservatism had flagged again—Carter had bested Ford, now Clinton had stemmed Bush. The following week, my doorbell rang. It was a wan Wednesday afternoon, the evanescence of a spent autumn. The election was over—my caller was likely a Jehovah's Witness.

I opened the door. The intruder was well-built—a muscular man in his forties with cropped (almost punk) blond hair. There was a scar above his temple. He was wearing a sport shirt and slacks. His shoes were casual but expensive—Bass, if I were guessing.

"Prof. Dassen?" he wondered.

"Yes, that's me."

"Professor, I'm sorry to bother you like this. But I'm

your son…Thor."

"I'm sorry…there must be some mistake. I have no son."

"Professor: Helen Hoffman lived. I'm her son. You're my father."

My knees wobbled—I lunged for the latch. "Come in," I managed weakly, but was becoming dizzy. I took his jacket, then motioned towards the living room. I struggled for composure. "Please sit down, er, Thor. May I offer you something? A cup of coffee?"

He sat in the armchair. "Coffee would be great—black, please."

I returned with a tray, placed it weakly on the table, then handed him his cup. I'd had time to prepare some lines. "The last thing I'd heard," I sighed, "Helen was at death's door." I took my cup and sat on the couch. I was queazy.

"Let's see. That'd've been October '44."

I recognized my nose on his face—the Warrior had arrived. "That sounds right."

"She died on Pearl Harbor Day, but they were able to save me."

'Save me'—I couldn't help thinking of the abortion debate. "You're a Sagittarius," I offered, not knowing what else to say.

He frowned, then sipped his coffee. "Don't mess with that stuff."

"Neither do I," I agreed.

He lifted a biscuit, then forced a grin. "So whaddya think, Pa—are we blood?"

I took a breath and hoped I could survive this. "Looks

that way," I admitted. Then gestured around. "Welcome home." Then was afraid some prof from the psych department would scold me for my coolness: "Run to him, kiss him, PROVE YOU'RE ALIVE, FRIEDRICH!" But instinct warned me just to be courteous.

He studied the archways. "Nice house."

"Julia Morgan, 1923."

"Famous architect?"

"Around here? Yeah. Beaux Arts graduate." He nodded, then put his cup down. The small talk was helping. "So, you live in California?"

He shook his head. "Virginia. Fairfax." Government. Middle-brow.

"Work for the Government?"

"Sometimes. Freelance. I'm what they call a soldier of fortune." He grinned.

I gulped. *"A mercenary?"*

"VP of a PMC—professional military company."

I was intrigued. "Really? Where've you guys been?"

"Congo, Haiti ..."

"Who pays you?"

"Governments…liberation movements ... COs."

"Cooperating—"

"Covert orgs. Fronts, basically."

"CIA?"

"Um, DGSE mostly ... M16…" The French, the Brits.

"What's the objective?"

He shrugged. "Always the same: 'minimum impact resolution.'"

"You get 'em to negotiate."

"Yep." He stretched his body. "The less conflict, the happier everyone is."

"Mmm. Well, that makes sense." I grabbed a biscuit. "So, er, you carry a 74 on your shoulder?"

He smiled, then propped his legs on the hassock. "I hung my gun up last year, Friedrich. I'm 48 years old."

"Yeah, you would be, wouldn't you?" A FedEx truck rumbled past the window. "So you're a supervisor?"

"Project manager. From my desk. In Virginia."

"Strategy, logistics…"

He nodded, then changed the subject. "And you're a prof at Cal State?"

"Yep, European history. How'd'ya know?" I refilled our cups.

"I know a lot about you."

"How come? Did you hire a detective?"

"I asked around."

The sun had set—I walked over and drew the drapes. Then lit the floor lamp. "All right, what do I teach?"

"20th century British, French, German…survey of Europe."

"Publication?"

"Uh…*From EEC to EU…The Politics of Recovery*— Wagner Prize for that one. '81, I think."

"Yeah, what else do you know?" I felt somewhat invaded.

"Married to Ingrid Scholl in '51, deceased '87. One daughter, Margaret, deceased '89." *(Is your secret safe, Maggie?)*

"Anything else?"

"You're popular at Hayward. Students voted you Fave Prof in '86."

"Well, you seemed to have summed up my half century."

He nodded, then changed the subject again. "How many bedrooms in this place?"

"Three. Would you like to peek upstairs?"

He nodded and we toured the house—bedrooms upstairs…downstairs office. "Ah, a Mac!" he congratulated me. "A man after my own heart."

"Absolutely," I confirmed. "I'd be lost without my mouse." We returned to the living room. "Would you care to stay for dinner, Thor?"

He shook his head. "Thanks, not really hungry. Ate at the trade show."

"In the city?"

"Yep, REPEX—er, Response Equipment Procurement."

"In *San Francisco?*"

"Sure. Lots of trade shows here. The Bay's a hub for contingency hardware."

I returned to nutrition. "Well, okay, how about some sourdough and cheese?"

"Sure—some bread, some cheese, glass of wine—sounds great."

"Okay, I'll light the fire." I slipped some Mozart into the player, then built a fire with a couple of logs. In the kitchen, I arranged some sourdough and gouda on a plate. When I returned, he was leafing through an issue of *Atlantic* and I wondered how exotic that was for him.

He pointed to the cover. "Used to be *Atlantic Monthly*?"

"Yeah, they changed a while back." I put down the tray and poured some wine.

"Yeah, well, this report on the Marines is bullshit."

"The Marines?—hadn't noticed that." I'd been drawn to the piece on the Nazis.

"Yeah, this DC report by this guy—" he fingered the page—"totally wrong."

"What's it say?"

"Oh, that the Army's phased out heavy artillery and is now on par with the Marines—you know, as an ex-ped force. In their fucking dreams the Army is expeditionary! Pure fiction."

"So he wants to retire the Marines?"

He nodded. "Yeah. Big mistake. The planet's three-quarters water—amphibious penetration's a discrete capability. And a vital one." He tossed the issue aside.

He layered some cheese on a bread slice, then took a bite. "Mmm. Excellent."

"Yeah, Dutch."

"Yeah, I was in Brussels last month. They served some killer cheese there. Said it was Eden or something."

"Edam, yeah."

"Dutch too, right?"

I nodded, then decided to pepper our exchange. "Do you guys ever turn down clients?"

"Oh, sure, lots of times. We won't assist embargoed nations, terrorist groups…what else?…uh, drug cartels, syndicates…"

"But you mentioned liberation movements."

"Yeah. Those are the tough ones. If they enjoy world support—like, say, East Timor—we'll work with 'em."

"I see."

"But not Israel."

"What's wrong with Israel?" Rabin had just been elected.

He shrugged. "We're a Christian outfit—Christian values. Scott feels the same way."

"Who's Scott?"

"CEO."

"But you'd work with Hindus, wouldn't you?"

"Yeah."

Uh oh, trouble. "Well, Hindus aren't Christian."

"No," he smiled. "But they're not Jews either." There was a faint expression of contempt on his face. For *me*, I thought—not the Jews.

I put my cup down and felt my pressure rising. "How come Jews offend you and Hindus don't?"

He smiled. "Well, there's this little matter of Jesus, isn't there?"

"You blame the Jews for the Crucifixion?"

"I don't care who crucified Him—I care who rejects Him."

"What about Hindus, Buddhists, Muslims?"

"It's not the same thing."

I looked away from him. *(Dammit, Maggie! The medication! Why'd ya quit?)*

"Look, Friedrich—"

"DON'T CALL ME THAT!" I snapped.

His faced tensed. "Do you want me to go?" Ingrid's

199

clock ticked—the one she bought in Geneva. I stared at the carpet. He was my surviving child. Nothing I might say or do could erase that fact.

"Don't go," I whispered, raising my hand. I looked up. "Let's work this out."

"I agree," he said softly.

I spoke from the heart. "Thor, I don't like the term antisemitism. The Arabs are Semitic-speakers—the term is silly. It was coined by some agitators in the 1870s. Actually, the earlier term *Judenhass*—'Jew hatred'—was more accurate."

"I don't hate anybody."

"Well, I prefer the term anti-Jewish."

"Fine."

My appetite was returning. I built a small sandwich and bit into it. Then sipped some wine. "So tell me why the Jewish attitude towards Christ is any different than the Hindu one...or the Buddhist one."

He finished his sandwich, then sighed. "Because the Jews are one of the pillars of the West. They're in the Inner Circle, so to speak. Their rejection counts."

"But the Jews don't exactly spend their days bad-mouthing Jesus."

"They don't have to. Their alienation speaks volumes."

I was losing patience. "Did you learn this crap in Teton? Who brought you up?"

He seemed to enjoy my annoyance. "Bud died in the shootout; Helen, after childbirth. Do you remember Karl and Edith?"

"Karl and Edith Mell? Sure. They weren't Nazis."

He glared at me. "Neither am I. Neither was Bud or Helen."

"Karl and Edith brought you up?"

"No, Rudy and Eva did—Karl's brother and his wife."

I sipped some coffee. "So you're offended by Jews."

"I'm not *offended*. You asked me why our firm doesn't work with Israel. I told you we're Christian."

"Israel was created by the U.N. as a refuge from persecution—persecution in the *Christian* world. Just in case you and your fascist buddies decide to fire up the ovens again."

He glared at me again. "I'm *not* fascist, Friedrich."

With a trembling hand, I pointed to Mother's portrait above the mantel. "Your grandmother *died* fighting fascism!"

"My grandma was a terrorist for Stalin."

"HOW DARE YOU RIDICULE HER! APOLOGIZE TO ME!"

He stood up with a dim smirk. There was no use pretending anymore—the Warrior was my nemesis. "I'm sorry, Friedrich," he said dutifully. "Helga was your mother. I was out of line." He retook his seat.

I sat down and shoved my plate away. "How do you know all this shit?"

"Your mother was controlled by the KGB. Her code name was *Cassandra*." Possible. KGB supplied her.

"How do you know this?"

"FIS." Last year Russia's Foreign Intelligence Service allowed U.S. scholars to review KGB archives. But how did Blond Boy get his mitts on 'em?

I was still furious. "What's your plan, Thor —extermination?"

He smiled incredulously. "God, Friedrich, you're convinced I'm Adolf Eichmann. And that's so wrong!"

"Well, your firm sells violence, imposes Christ—"

"We don't force Christ on anybody. We simply believe the world will be at peace when everyone accepts Jesus."

"And if they don't, your buddies will force 'em to!"

"No! We defend civilization from terrorists, syndicates, Marxists. We believe that—left to its own devices—without coercion from gangsters, agitators—people will, in the end, come to Christ. The world will be a Christian commonwealth."

"Look, Thor—what's your family name, by the way—Metts?"

"No, Hoffman."

"Thor Hoffman?"

He nodded. "Thorstein Gunther Hoffman. Yep."

"Well, look, this obsession of yours—"

"It's not an obsession."

"Sure it is. You said it yourself: Jewish 'alienation'— their mere *being* grates on you!"

"I didn't say that."

"You said their 'alienation from Christ speaks volumes.'"

"I said it *counts*. It makes an *impression*."

"So your outfit would like to get rid of them?"

"No!"

"How do you get a Christian Commonwealth with 18 million Jews on the planet?"

He tried to reason with me. "Nobody is persecuted. Everyone comes to it voluntarily. I mean, by your standards, Friedrich, the *Vatican* is anti-Jewish!"

"On a bad day, yes."

"That's ridiculous!"

"Tell that to the victims of the Inquisition." He shook his head incredulously. But I kept charging. "Look, it's obsessive to be so…*hyper-conscious* of another group. Leave them alone—they're not bothering you."

"They *are* bothering me."

"On a personal level? Or collectively?"

"Symbolically."

"That's your problem, not theirs."

He shook his head. "All I can tell you is that many people in my generation feel like I do."

"Feel how? Like they can't live with Jews?"

"IT'S EVERYWHERE, THEIR PARADIGM! Freud's psychology, Einstein's relativity—"

"Heisenberg and Schrödinger weren't Jewish. Quantum mechanics is more subversive than relativity!"

But he wasn't listening. "The liberalism, the welfare state, the endless debate, the rationality, the intellect—"

I raised my hands. "Whoa! This is exactly the Nazi fallacy: 'Jewish physics,' 'Jewish psychology,' 'Jewish politics.' Liberalism isn't Jewish. It derives from England—the Magna Carta, John Locke, Jeremy Bentham. 'Greatest good for the greatest number' wasn't written in Hebrew!"

"But the Jews have glommed on to it! We're suffocating in liberalism!"

"But the Jews aren't the only ones 'glomming' on, as you put it—so are your German cousins. And the Japanese. After Hitler, Stalin, and Tojo, liberalism's lookin' pretty good."

"You can have it."

"What's wrong with it?" I walked to the hearth and fed the fire. I was starting to feel smug. And enjoying it.

He raised his voice as I fiddled with the kindling. "It *lies* about the world. It creates the impression that a successful species goes to school, does its homework, gets a law degree, and spends the rest of its life defending its interests—in Congress, on campus, in court, in the media. THAT'S NOT REALITY!"

I returned to the couch. "No? What is?"

"A cold, ruthless, dangerous universe…where talent and resources are precious…where there are few winners and many losers…where success is secured—*through constant risk*—by talent, wealth, and power."

"What kind of risk?"

He counted on his fingers: "Financial, corporal, genetic—entrepreneurial, military, reproductive."

I smelled racism again. "What's reproductive risk?"

"The possibility that genetic talent might be overwhelmed in the pool."

"You sound like the Republicans—Hispanics overrunning California!"

"It's not race, it's not ethnicity—it's *talent*."

"As if that can be inherited! Look at *you*!"

He frowned. Then paused. "Look, Friedrich, you asked me to sit down and work this out. You're my father, you're an old man—I agreed. But if you're going to insult me, I'm going to have to leave."

I raised my hand in concession. "Yeah, and I don't want you to." He nodded. But I wouldn't let up. "So where does Christ come in?"

"Christ is the Light at the End of the Tunnel."

"Then why's it so hard for a rich man to get into heaven?"

"It's not."

"Christ was wrong?"

"The First Coming was a demonstration of what the Kingdom of Heaven might be. It was rejected. Humanity has to work itself back to that point."

"To what point?"

"The opportunity to realize the Kingdom. I hope we get it right."

"So this is essentially Calvinist Darwinism—" he nodded—"with an anti-Jewish twist."

"You can't be Christian and Jewish at the same time."

I raised my index finger. "No, but you can be an enlightened Christian, a tolerant one."

He scowled. "Well, you don't want to be so open-minded your brains fall out."

"What about a Jewish entrepreneur?" I goaded.

"A mixed bag. The enterprise is noble, the Judaism isn't."

"So if you could take an executive on a life raft, you'd choose the Christian one."

"Maybe."

"Probably." I chuckled. "I'd hate to be the Jewish one!"

It was time to sum things up. "I don't know, Thor, I think you've got a psychological problem. You're bitter and you project your bitterness on Jews. It's not even specific Jews you have a problem with—their *aura* makes you uncomfortable."

"I didn't say 'aura.' I said 'paradigm.'"

"However you put it, the fact that you're dealing collectively—symbolically—is a sign your subconscious is involved. It's a sign of paranoia."

"You're saying I'm crazy?" The tension was mounting again.

"Have you seen a therapist?"

"I'M CRAZY?" he exploded. "You come to America a Marxist with a swastika on your lapel, you knock up a Nationalist for kicks while your 'heroic' Mom is being gang-banged by the Gestapo. (You're, of course, not at all perturbed by this, so long as you're getting your rocks off.) Then to honor your Mom's memory, you betray the mother of your child to the Iron Heel, who for its own reasons takes the opportunity to murder her, despite some queasiness about shooting a pregnant woman."

"That's not fair."

"Wait! Her son survives, no thanks to Dad, who despite the fact he returns to the West and eventually pulls down 100K, can't be bothered to admit paternity, pay child support...nor even, God forbid, mail a Christmas present once in a while. The kid grows up in a Nationalist home with the comforting thought that his father set up the murder of his mother to honor the death of a Stalinist..."

I raised my hand.

"No, wait! In his 40s, the son, who has somehow managed to find Christ through all this, *forgives* his Pa and pays the old man a visit, only to be accused of being a dumb Nazi…this, despite the fact he took shrapnel in his brain while defending Aristide—a significant improvement on advancing democracy, one would think, than his father's military career which consisted of—let's be frank—assisting Adolf Hitler's conquest of Africa." He looked me in the eyes. "And *I'm* the one who's crazy? I think you've got a few problems of your own, Daddy."

We stared into each other's eyes. I remembered searching the eyes of Ingrid's Doberman in Paris—cavernous, ancient, ruthless—as Kim's Militia stormed Seoul. But my son's were empty.

I cleared my throat. "You defended Aristide?"

"Yeah."

"During the coup?" He nodded. "I would've thought you'd've sided with the junta."

"The *Macoute?* Those Voodoo thugs? They shot priests in their beds." Ah, of course—Christian defense.

I sighed. "*Ja*, the world's a complicated place."

He stretched out his hand.

"I can't shake your hand, Thor."

He quickly withdrew it. "Why not?" His face was tense.

"I'm not going to make peace without Jews in the room."

"You want me to bring a Jew here?"

"Now *I'm* being symbolic. I'm not going to befriend you while you wish another people ill. No matter how pure your motives."

He laughed contemptuously. "If you like them so much, maybe you should become one!"

"Nah, not my style. I'll just spend the rest of my life tripping up Christian fascists like you."

"I'm your son," he said softly.

"Uh huh," I agreed.

He stood up and shouted at me: "From the day I was conceived, you wanted me dead!" His voice turned tearful. "Admit it, you bastard! If you could've flushed me out of her womb, you'd've done it! Well, guess what, Professor? I'm gonna live to a fuckin' hundred no matter what you say!"

"I hope you do."

"JUST SAY IT—YOU HATE ME!"

"I don't." But he'd grabbed his jacket and slammed the door.

♦

"Maggi, take your medication."

"What's the point, Fred?"

"You're a young woman—you have everything to live for."

"Without time, there's nothin', Daddy."

"Whaddya talkin' about, honey? You've got plenty of time. You'll meet another guy, raise a family—"

"There is no time! It's an illusion. Just another bedtime story."

"So what if there is or not? You're free to live, fall in love, win the Nobel. C'mon, Magpie—enjoy!"

"That's not what you wrote in your notebook."

"What notebook?"

"From the prison camp."

"You read THAT*?"*

"Mm hm. Found it in the attic."

"Sweetheart…that was during the War. Everyone was nuts then. Loco in the coco."

"But not my Daddy! You were right on!"

"Ach, formulas—they don't mean a thing. Life's all that matters, Magpie—the axiom of the heart."

♦

I walked over to the bookcase and removed a copy of *The Young Marx*. Mother used to say the *Manifesto* was political, *Kapital* was economic, but the "Manuscripts"—they were *geistlich* [spiritual]. They were written in Paris in 1844, a year after Marx left Germany. He was only twenty-six.

I sat before the embers and reviewed his components of "alienation." They included:

1) *declining purchasing power*—no longer being able to afford the products your fellow proles make;

2) *demotion to servitude*—being reduced to the status of flunky;

3) *the devaluation of craftsmanship*—being forced to forsake personalized and/or elegant production;

4) *atomization*—being forced to compete with fellow proles as a discrete commodity…rather than fraternally uniting with them.

Stalin's father was an unemployed shoemaker, who regularly beat his son with vodka on his breath. Stalin's mother groomed him for the priesthood. Rankled by his father's brutality and his mother's moralism, he turned to Bolshevism in 1903. In the mid-'20s, he wrested power from Lenin's heirs—Trostky, Kamenev, Zinovyev. In '32 his wife Nadezhda committed suicide upon learning of genocide in the Ukraine. (Her student informants were fingered and shot.) From '35-'38, the 'Boss' executed over ten percent of his subjects—some twenty million Soviets. Their crime was 'deviation.'

Chinese communism has been less bloody but Tiananmen Square betrayed its legacy. Cuban communism has delivered social benefits, but its oligarchic control over politics, economics, education, and culture is reminiscent of Stalin. *Viva Hidalgo.*

Where did Marxism go bad? With Lenin! In his pamphlet, *What is to be Done?*, he proposed a proletarian dictatorship. That sharpened the Party strategically but doomed his regime to oligarchy.

Yet, despite the tyranny practiced in his name, the vision of Young Marx remains instructive. It's a call for equitable distribution of wealth, so that farm workers, as well as engineers, might afford decent housing, healthcare and education. It demands an egalitarian workplace, so that managers will no longer humble their charges. It urges a return to an intimate interaction between producer and product. It fosters solidarity between working people.

In his recent encyclical, the Pope supports the struggle against the "absolute predominance of capital." While he validates private property and individual profit, he also champions "human and moral factors...which, in the long term, are at least equally important"—including "service" to the "whole of society" and rights that stem from "essential dignity...It is possible for financial accounts to be in order and yet for people...to be humiliated and their dignity offended."

Nearly a century and a half after the "Manuscripts," a consensus looms between the Vatican and Marx. It suggests a system of humane enterprise, where individual talent, innovation, risk, rights, dignity, and discipline might coexist with social welfare.

Thor will be fine. Having denounced me, he's free to befriend me. Every infant rejects his father. The toddler then admires the man. Thor never had that chance.

But in time, he and Judy will visit in summer. They'll help thin lettuce in the yard. We'll cheer the A's from the bleachers. One afternoon, as the fog hurtles in, I'll confide to them I've sold the house.

Mother stares down from the mantel. The glow of the hearth turns Karl's face orange. I've traveled from *Die Jugund* to the Antlers to Cal State. A photo of Adlai still hangs in my office. But I'm moving to a bolder vision. Finally I'm my mother's son.

Author's Historical Postscript

Split Creek extrapolates its plot from historical fact. But readers deserve to know which elements are factual and which are extrapolated...and, if extrapolated, how radically.

The following addendum aims to briefly acquaint readers with the history of German Communism; internment of German POWs in the U.S.; U.S. fascism and domestic wartime sabotage; and the Manhattan Project. It also considers whether an atemporal cosmology—such as the one apparently found in one of Dassen's notebooks from Camp Roberts—could have been deduced during World War II.

GERMAN COMMUNIST PARTY

There were between 300,000 and 360,000 members of the German Communist Party when Hitler acceded to power in 1933. Over the next six and a half years, the Nazis interned nearly 140,000 and may have murdered as many as 20,000.[8] But after the Hitler-Stalin Pact was signed in mid-'39, an estimated 80-90 percent of interned members were freed.

[8] Horst Duhnke, *Die KPD von 1933 bis 1945* (Cologne: Kiepenheuer & Witsch, 1972)

After the Pact as well, sons of Communists who weren't Jewish, Gypsy, homosexual, or rejected physically were welcomed into the armed forces as enlistees or, if qualified, officers.

During the war, some German Communists were active in the Underground. After Germany invaded the Soviet Union, at least nine major communist networks were exposed and its leaders executed; Communists also assisted some non-communist groups. As many as 4000 Communist civilians may have been executed during the war.

GERMAN POWs IN THE U.S.

Between May 1942–June 1946, over 370,000 German, 50,000 Italian, and 5000 Japanese POWs were interned in the U.S. The Pentagon's Provost Marshal General administered some 155 camps, each containing between 2000 and 4000 soldiers or officers. Each site typically boasted three or four "branch" camps, i.e. remote operations close to orchards, cropfields, mines, quarries, etc. Camps were mostly located in the South, Plains, and Great Lakes; but over a dozen main camps operated in the Deep West.

As cited in the novel, prior to mid-'44, Nazi NCOs may have either murdered, or induced the suicides, of some 250 of their fellow soldiers in the camps, presumably for political deviation.[9] Later that year, the Penta-

---

[9] Arnold Krammer, *Nazi Prisoners of War in America* (Lanham, MD: Scarborough House, 1996), p. 173

gon began to quarantine these enforcers in special camps and systemically introduce the Denazification Program described in *Split Creek*.

U.S. FASCISM AND WARTIME SABOTAGE

The notion of wartime subversion in the Deep West is historically inaccurate. There were certainly small fascist groups in the U.S. throughout the 1930s but they were based in Massachusetts, New York, Pennsylvania, West Virginia, District of Columbia, Michigan, Indiana, and the West Coast—not in the Rockies or Plains. Indeed, as implied in the novel's dedication, the Deep West's interaction with fascism was apparently confined to valorous opposition to the Axis via the U.S. military.

The novel sets wartime subversion in the Deep West only because it views the region as an epigrammatic American landscape: "...purple mountain majesties above the fruited plain." In the '40s, America was a place that harbored remnants of fascist resentment but, as a whole, either rejected fascism outright...or, like protagonist Dassen, eventually reached that conclusion.

The idea of pockets of fascist sentiment among a sliver of German-Americans is more plausible. As late as 1939, the Nazi German-American Bund boasted 20,000 members. The more elite Steuben Society retained 100,000 members, although it's doubtful its rank and file were typically fascist; all that may be safely said is that the society's leaders were fellow travelers of National Socialism until the mid-'30s.[10] But there's no evidence of German-American fascism after Pearl Harbor. And, of course, German-Americans as a whole (over a quarter of the U.S.) were nearly uniformly loyal to Uncle Sam, with an estimated quarter million serving honorably in the armed forces.

Is there any evidence, then, of *any* U.S. fascism—let alone sabotage—after Pearl Harbor? Documentation is ambiguous. At the end of '43, the FBI reported 1300 incidents of domestic sabotage since Pearl Harbor.[11] But there's no evidence any was politically inspired.

As cited in the novel, however, there were two major plans for domestic sabotage that were coincident with the expansion of Nazi Germany—one executed in 1939, the second aborted in 1942:

•*Railroad Sabotage:* Some three weeks before Hitler invaded Poland, saboteurs queered the Southern Pacific tracks in Nevada, plunging the *City of San Francisco* streamliner into a canyon, killing over twenty passengers and crew. The Interstate Commerce Commission found sabotage, but SP detectives and the FBI never found the perpetrators. Consequently, there's no evidence the attack was politically motivated, and the case remains open.

---

[10] See: T.H. Tetens, *Pan-Germanism in the United States: An Expose on the Activities of the Steuben Society* (New York: Society for Prevention of World War III, 1946?)

[11] "FBI Finds Sabotage in 1300 Cases in War," *N.Y. Times*, December 29, 1943, p. 10; see also: "Finds 1736 Cases of Sabotage in U.S.," July 16, 1944, p. 7

•*Industrial Sabotage:* In June '42, a German-American, George John Dasch, led a covert German operation against the U.S.: it landed a team of four operatives off the coast of Long Island and another off the coast of northern Florida. The teams were equipped with explosives; their mission was to sabotage factories, utilities, and depots. Soon after arrival, Dasch betrayed the operation to the FBI. Six of his comrades were executed that August; Dasch and a seventh were pardoned, then deported, in '48. The Pentagon maintains Dasch was not a double agent.

MANHATTAN PROJECT

It is well known that various U.S. and U.K. Communists slipped information about the Manhattan Project to Soviet agents prior to Hiroshima. But did U.S. fascists learn about the Project beforehand, as the novel suggests?

In reviewing the Project, the former National Counterintelligence Center noted the effort was "vulnerable to espionage and sabotage."[12] After Hiroshima, the Associated Press reported that information about the Project had been specifically sought by German intelligence.[13] But there's no evidence that U.S. fascists knew of the Manhattan Project before Hiroshima.

---

[12] Frank J. Rafalko, ed., *Counterintelligence Reader: World War II* (Washington: National Counterintelligence Center, 1998)

[13] "All Foreign Sabotage of Atomic Bomb Failed," *N.Y. Times*, August 9, 1945, p. 6

ATEMPORAL COSMOLOGY

Atemporal cosmology—cosmology that denies fundamental spacetime—has been formally proposed over the past twenty-five years by at least two physicists in London: Drs. David Bohm in 1980 and Julian Barbour in 1999.[14] Barbour, for his part, claims he's been influenced by the implications of the Wheeler-DeWitt Equation (1967) and Bell's Inequalities (1964) regarding the Einstein-Podolsky-Rosen Paradox (1935). But it seems possible to deduce atemporality from earlier influences, i.e. Machian mechanics (1883), the Schrödinger Stationary Equation (1926), Dirac's Transformation Theory (1930), and the EPR Paradox itself.

FOOTNOTES

All footnotes have been interpolated by the author and are historically accurate. Those appearing in Dassen's narrative are signed [VOB].

---

[14] See: David Bohm, *Wholeness and the Implicate Order* (London: Routledge, 1980); Julian Barbour, *The End of Time* (London: Oxford, 1999)

Further Reading

GERMAN COMMUNISM (1933-45)

Duhnke, Horst, *German Communism in the Nazi Era*. Unpublished dissertation. Berkeley: University of California, 1964.

U.S. FASCISM (1933-45)

Carlson, John Roy, *Under Cover: My Four Years in the Nazi Underworld of America*. Cleveland: World, 1943. (John Roy Carlson was the pseudonym of George Derounian, brother of former U.S. Rep. Steven Derounian [R-NY]. George Derounian initially covered U.S. fascism for *Fortune*.)

Rogge, O. John, *Official German Report*. New York: Thomas Yoseloff, 1961.
(Belated publication of wartime report on U.S. fascism by Asst. U.S. Attorney General.)

GERMAN POWs IN THE U.S. (1942-46)

Bailey, Ronald H, "A Pragmatic Lenience," pp. 156-69 in his: *Prisoners of War*. New York: Time-Life Books, 1981.

Fincher, Jack, "'America beats by far anything,' said the

ex-POW." *Smithsonian* 26 (June 1995): 126-43.

Gansberg, Judith M., *Stalag: USA*. New York: Crowell, 1977.

Krammer, Arnold, *Nazi Prisoners of War in America*. Lanham, MD: Scarborough House, 1996.

Deep West

Bangerter, Lowell A., "German Prisoners of War in Wyoming." *Journal of German-American Studies* 14 (1979): 65-123.

Horner, Helmut, *A German Odyssey: Journal of a German Prisoner of War*. Golden, CO: Fulcrum Publishing, 1991.

Jardon, Jean and Dollie Iberlin, *The White Root*. Self-published. Buffalo, WY: 1988.
(A history of German-Russian immigrants to Wyoming's Clear Creek Valley, including a passing reference [pp. 83, 85] to German POWs assigned to their farms in 1945.)

Powell, Allan Kent, *Splinters of a Nation: German Prisoners of War in Utah*. Salt Lake City: University of Utah Press, 1989.

NATIVE AMERICANS: U.S. PLAINS

Densmore, Frances, "Use of Music by the American Indians," in: *Music & Medicine*, Dorothy Schullian and Max Schoen, eds., pp. 25-46. New York: Henry Schuman, 1948.

Laubin, Reginald and Gladys, *Indian Dances of North*

America. Norman, OK: University of Oklahoma Press, 1977.

Yellowtail, "Sweat Lodge" in: *Yellowtail: Crow Medicine Man and Sun Dance Chief,* an autobiography told to Michael Oren Fitzgerald, pp. 106-14. Norman, OK: University of Oklahoma Press, 1991.

Past Acclaim for V.O. Blum's Fiction

Equator: The Story and the Letters, Blum's first novel:

Blum has a real talent for dialogue and narrative flow. The Letters are great.

—Nancy J. Peters
Executive Editor
City Lights Books

"Sperm Boy," the lead novella in Blum's collection, ***Sunbelt Stories:***

Hello to anybody who's thinking about reading V.O. Blum's "Sperm Boy." This is a faraway drummer calling with a message for same. Read it. But if you can't read it, then at least buy it. Reason is this—some of the revenue must make its way to Blum and, in so doing, will help put chicken and peas on his/her table, from which nutrition there could issue nutriment, in due-er than most courses, to the body of the national literature. No life without renewal, right? Or are you looking for an argument with nature?

—Gordon Lish

At first I resisted this raunchy comic sad heap of a short novel—aging woman with cancer hires young Albanian Catholic to provide a sperm cure?—but then, but then…V.O. Blum brings valuable news of the world through a tale told with wit and chagrin.

—Herbert Gold

"Sperm Boy" is an evocative piece on the real source of the life force.

—Vidura Le Feuvre
Former Director
Findhorn Foundation
Forres, Scotland